The sound of a snapping twig startled her and Emma's heart pounded in alarm.

And then she saw him. He moved out of the shadows and for a moment he stood silhouetted in the doorway of the gazebo.

Ash.

Slowly he stepped inside. She couldn't see his face clearly, but she knew that he was staring at her. She felt the heat of his gaze pierce the walls she'd built around her heart, and it frightened her. Excited her. She hardly dared breathe for fear he might disappear again.

He moved toward her and she closed her eyes.

"You remembered," she whispered.

DOUBLE LIFE

AMANDA STEVENS

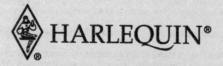

HARLEQUIN®

TORONTO • NEW YORK • LONDON
AMSTERDAM • PARIS • SYDNEY • HAMBURG
STOCKHOLM • ATHENS • TOKYO • MILAN • MADRID
PRAGUE • WARSAW • BUDAPEST • AUCKLAND

ISBN-13: 978-0-373-88728-6
ISBN-10: 0-373-88728-0

DOUBLE LIFE

Copyright © 2006 by Marilyn Medlock Amann

ABOUT THE AUTHOR

Amanda Stevens is a bestselling author of over thirty novels of romantic suspense. In addition to being a Romance Writers of America RITA® Award finalist, she is also the recipient of awards in Career Achievement in Romantic/Mystery and Career Achievement in Romantic/Suspense from *Romantic Times BOOKclub*. She currently resides in Texas. To find out more about past, present and future projects, please visit her Web site at www.amandastevens.com.

Books by Amanda Stevens

HARLEQUIN INTRIGUE
737—HIS MYSTERIOUS WAYS*
759—SILENT STORM*
777—SECRET PASSAGE*
796—UNAUTHORIZED PASSION
825—INTIMATE KNOWLEDGE
834—MATTERS OF SEDUCTION
862—GOING TO EXTREMES
882—THE EDGE OF ETERNITY
930—SECRETS OF HIS OWN
954—DOUBLE LIFE

*Quantum Men

CAST OF CHARACTERS

Emma Novick—Recovering from a brutal attack, Emma returns to her childhood home, only to be caught up in a web of lies and deceit that could destroy her dreams...and her life.

Ash Corbett—Twelve years ago the heir to the Corbett fortune took off without a word to anyone. Now he's back, but is he the real Ash Corbett...or a cunning impostor?

Helen Corbett—The matriarch of the Corbett family will do anything to keep Emma away from her grandson.

Wesley Corbett—A generous man with a dangerous secret.

Brad Corbett—He's lived in his brother's shadow for far too long.

Pamela Corbett—Wesley's cold, greedy wife.

Lynette Corbett—Brad's wife is afraid of the Corbett secrets.

Maris Corbett—The only Corbett daughter, she appears to be genuinely happy to have Ash home...but is it just an act?

Rick Bledsoe—A county sheriff's deputy who makes a surprising confession.

Shell Island—As a kid, Emma had a strange premonition about the island. A few years later, the bodies of six young women who had been brutally murdered were uncovered there. And now the island is luring Emma back....

Chapter One

Nestled in a horseshoe-shaped cove on the Gulf of Mexico, Jacob's Pass, Texas, was a gorgeous little town with a dark past.

By day, the pastel buildings shimmered like jewels in the heat, but come twilight, a pervasive uneasiness settled over the picturesque landscape. Doors were locked, window blinds drawn. The entire community seemed to hold a collective breath as if waiting anxiously for dawn to come and banish the night creatures back to their holes. It had been that way for over thirty years...ever since the first body had been found.

Emma Novick glanced at the sky as she strode toward the pier, where she'd left her car. The day was slipping away. Already the sun had started to sink below the treetops and in another hour, dusk would be upon her.

But it wasn't the old murders that made Emma worry about the coming dark.

She fingered the scar at the base of her neck as a chill slid over her. Sometimes when she lay alone in her bed at night, she could still feel her assailant's hands on her body, his hot breath on her face. But it did no good to dwell on her fears. The attack had been over a year ago. It was over and done with. She'd survived the brutal assault and her testimony had sent the perpetrator to prison. He wouldn't hurt her, or anyone else, ever again.

The only thing she had to be afraid of now was her loneliness. And the gnawing dread deep inside that she would grow old alone, that she would live a life devoid of passion and love because she couldn't let go of the past.

Couldn't stop dreaming about a man who no longer existed. May *never* have existed except in a young moonstruck mind.

What frightened Emma even more were those rare occasions when she took a long, hard look at herself in the mirror and allowed herself to witness the passage of time. She was still a young woman, not even thirty, but she thought she would be married with a family of her own by now.

Instead, she spent her days catering to the

whims of her tyrannical employer, whose sole joy in life was making those around her miserable.

At the thought of Helen Corbett, Emma hurried her steps. She hadn't meant to linger so long in town, but her outings were few and far between these days and the June weather was so perfect. Hot, yes, but a hint of rain cooled the breeze that blew in from the gulf.

Still, Emma knew she should have headed back hours ago. Helen would be upset by her tardiness, and when Helen Corbett got upset, there would be hell to pay.

But her brief escape had been worth it, Emma decided. With the wind whipping at her skirt and tossing her dark hair, she felt younger and more carefree than she had in years.

She supposed it was silly to feel old at twenty-nine, but on days when Helen was especially difficult, Emma swore she could actually feel her youth waning.

She considered herself strong and resilient—she would never have returned to Jacob's Pass otherwise, no matter how sweet the deal—but Helen Corbett could try the patience of a saint.

Always difficult, the woman's disposition had deteriorated as rapidly as her health.

She'd never quite recovered from a stroke two years ago that had left her confined to a wheelchair for the better part of six months.

It had only been through sheer determination and a plain old stubborn streak that she could now get around with a cane and her speech patterns were almost back to normal, although her voice had grown quite feeble in the past year.

She was thin and birdlike, but her appearance had always been deceptive. Beneath the frail-looking demeanor were a backbone of steel and a heart of stone. Helen Corbett was not a kind woman, but there had always been something about her that Emma admired and respected.

And, of course, at one time they'd shared something in common—a complete and utter devotion to Ash Corbett.

Helen's grandson had been the apple of her eye and the love of Emma's life until he'd taken off without a word twelve years ago. Neither woman had been the same since he left, and perhaps that was why Emma could exercise more restraint in dealing with the cantankerous Helen than her own family could. Emma understood better than anyone how desolate and bitter life could be without Ash.

Lifting her face to the warm sea breeze, she paused to admire the scenery as she neared the pier. The tiny cove was dotted with fishing vessels and motorboats putting back in for the day and she loved to watch them. Loved imagining herself at the prow of some great ship, arms spread wide as Ash's powerful hands held her steady and safe.

But she wouldn't think any more about Ash today. What was the point? He'd been gone for over a decade. Dead for all she knew. He'd left town one night without looking back…just a few short weeks after the gruesome discovery was made on Shell Island.

Not that there was any connection. No matter the rumors at the time, Emma refused to believe that Ash had been a part of that depravity, that…evil.

Besides, he'd only been a baby when the original murder occurred, and Emma was a firm believer in the one-killer theory. The other scenario—that two brutal psychopaths had preyed on the same tiny community eighteen years apart—was unfathomable.

The first victim had been a young high school teacher named Mary Ferris. She'd been missing for nearly two weeks when her mutilated body had been found in the cove.

Faced with a jittery community, the local police chief had insisted that the murder was an anomaly. The poor woman had either fallen victim to a jealous lover or a deranged drifter passing through town. There was no need for mass panic and, anxious to believe they were still safe in their homes, the townspeople had eagerly accepted the explanation.

And then eighteen years later, another mutilated body had been found on Shell Island by some teenagers who'd gone there to party.

A search of the tiny islet had turned up six more bodies in varying degrees of decomposition. A forensic anthropologist called in to help with the identification had concluded that the women had died within a five-year period of one another.

Four of the victims were from Houston, two from nearby Corpus Christi, and one from farther south in Brownsville. Only one victim remained unidentified, and she had apparently been dead longer than the others.

According to the forensic anthropologist, all of the women had been in their mid- to late-twenties and all of them had been tortured.

Emma had been seventeen at the time, just starting to spread her wings, and she vividly recalled the terror that gripped the community in the aftermath of the discovery. Her father, like every other parent in Jacob's Pass, had clamped down on her extracurricular activities to the point of suffocation. If not for her secret assignations with Ash, Emma would have gone stir-crazy.

But as close as she and Ash were at that time, she'd never told him of her deepest fear…that whatever had happened to those poor women on Shell Island could have been prevented by her.

Perhaps it was hubris on her part to take on that kind of responsibility, but Emma had known something terrible had occurred on the island long before the first body was ever found. She'd been gripped with a terrible feeling of foreboding the moment she first set foot on the beach.

If only she'd said something then, but who would have believed a twelve-year-old kid? The authorities would have chalked it up to an overactive imagination and maybe they would have been right. Maybe what she felt that day had been nothing more than the culmination of the legends she'd heard all her life.

Those legends were the reason she'd gone to the island in the first place. Her seventh-grade class had been studying local culture and she'd badgered her father into borrowing a boat and taking her out to the island because it was so steeped in history and folklore.

Until the 1950s, Shell Island had been inhabited by a handful of families who, like the Amish, eschewed modern conveniences, but one by one they'd migrated to the mainland until all that remained on the tiny clump of land were the abandoned homes and an old stone church.

For a while, rumors of dark ceremonies and ritualistic worship had followed the inhabitants to the mainland, but once the families moved on, the stories were eventually forgotten.

Except for teenagers looking to party and the occasional ghost hunter or archaeologist, no one ever went to the island anymore. Legend had it that the island was an old Indian burial ground, and at the time, Emma thought all the talk among her classmates had probably fueled her imagination. She hadn't said anything to her father about her uneasiness, but as they'd walked through the deserted houses, she'd become more and more agitated.

And when they reached the old church, she hadn't been able to go inside. She couldn't physically make herself step through the door. It was as if some dark force held her back.

Five years later, the first body had been found in that same church. Emma had no way of knowing whether one of the poor victims had been inside the day she stood trembling on the threshold, or whether her trepidation had been a premonition of what was to come.

She hadn't talked about that experience to anyone, even Ash. Especially not to Ash, because she hadn't wanted him to laugh at her. Hadn't wanted him to think of her as an immature child prone to exaggerations. Bad enough that he'd caught her spying on him.

Tucking her short hair behind her ears, Emma searched the water. This time of day, Shell Island was barely a speck against the deepening horizon, but she spotted it easily because she knew exactly where to look.

Funny how after all this time, when she let herself reminisce, that same sensation of dread came back to haunt her.

"EMMA! EMMA NOVICK!"

Emma had no idea how long she'd been standing there gazing out at the island when she heard her name being called.

She whirled and saw a young woman on the other side of the street waving frantically to get her attention. Emma lifted her hand in response, then watched as the blonde sprinted across the street in front of oncoming traffic.

"Watch out!" Emma called.

With a little shriek, Laney Carroway jumped to the curb just as a car swished past her. Then she gave a breathless laugh. "Whew, that was a close one!"

"Are you okay?" Emma asked in concern.

Instead of answering, Laney lifted her sunglasses and gave Emma a quick once-over. "So it really is you," she said almost in wonder. "When I first spotted you over here, I almost didn't recognize you. You look so different."

"I'm wearing my hair shorter," Emma murmured. She didn't like talking about her appearance.

"You've lost weight, too." Laney continued to study her. "If I hadn't heard you were back in town, I never would have known it was you."

Emma smiled. "It's been awhile. I guess we've all changed."

"Not me," Laney declared. "I look exactly the same as the day we graduated from high school. I haven't aged a bit."

She was joking, of course, but her freckled complexion and impish features did make her look about fifteen. She had a young outlook on life, too. Emma had always admired Laney's sunny personality. Good humor seemed to radiate from her green eyes.

Emma, on the other hand…

The mental reflection she conjured up didn't please her so she exiled her image to the far recesses of her mind. The years hadn't been as kind to her. Loneliness had taken a toll, she feared. And so had the attack.

"I heard a few weeks ago that you were back," Laney was saying, a subtle accusation creeping into her tone. "But I refused to believe it. I kept thinking that if you really had moved back to Jacob's Pass, I'd be the first one to know. Me being your best friend and all."

"I'm sorry, Laney. I've been meaning to call ever since I got back, but it's been pretty hectic. The move was kind of sudden, and I had so many things to take care of…" Emma trailed off with an apologetic shrug.

Laney nodded. "I imagine that old battle-ax keeps you hopping, too." She pushed her sunglasses to the top of her head. The blond wisps that escaped and framed her face made her look even younger. "What's she like these days? She was a regular tyrant when she had to come to the hospital for physical therapy after her stroke. I never personally had to deal with her, thank God, but I heard some of the other nurses complaining about her impossible demands. I have to give the devil her due, though. Even her own doctors thought she'd never walk again, but she showed them. She showed everyone."

"She's an amazingly strong woman," Emma agreed.

"That doesn't answer my question," Laney said. "How is she to work for?"

"She's…challenging," Emma said after a slight hesitation and Laney laughed.

"You're much too tactful. Me? I have no trouble calling 'em as I see 'em, but you were always too much of a lady to speak your mind. I see you haven't changed in that regard."

"Well, she is my employer," Emma said carefully. Unless she wanted to find herself out of a job, a certain amount of discretion was warranted.

Laney's expression sobered. "Why *did* you come back here, Em? Last I heard you had a great job with some Fortune 500 company in Dallas. You must have been doing really well for yourself, and everyone knows that Helen Corbett is so tight she squeaks when she walks. So don't tell me she made you an offer you couldn't refuse because I won't believe it. There had to be something else."

"There was." Not that Emma owed anyone an explanation for her move. Still, she knew people were bound to be curious so she had a ready answer. "Dad's getting on in years and there's no one but me to look after him. And I needed a change."

Understanding softened Laney's smile. "Now, *that* I can appreciate. I'm kind of in a rut myself. Sometimes I get so bored with my life in this Podunk town, I could just scream. Which is why I had a hard time understanding why you'd leave the big D to come back here, but I forgot about your dad. He had a heart attack last year, didn't he? That must have been a scary time for both of you."

Scary and difficult trying to take care of him while holding down a full-time job and dealing with the aftermath of her assault. There were days when Emma hadn't wanted to crawl out of bed, but somehow she'd made it through the ordeal. She was stronger and healthier now, but facing her own mortality had changed her. Some days it was almost as if she were a stranger in her own body, and she'd grown more and more restless with each passing day.

And then a chance meeting with Wesley Corbett, Helen's son, in the lobby of her office building had precipitated a bit of soul-searching. Emma had found herself dwelling on all the loose ends in her life that needed to be resolved, one way or another.

After exchanging pleasantries, Wesley had left his card, telling her to call if she ever needed a job.

Two days later, Emma had contacted him at his office in Corpus Christi, but his offer had taken her completely by surprise. Rather than an administrative position similar to the one she held with her current firm, he'd wanted her to become Helen Corbett's personal assistant and companion.

He'd told her that his mother no longer went into the office, but she still had her fingers in the business. She required someone to act as her liaison in board meetings, someone other than family that she could trust. She also needed someone besides the servants to talk to. He was worried that she was alone too much and that her solitude was causing her mind to slip.

"Emma?"

She snapped herself back to the present conversation. "I'm sorry. You were saying?"

"Your dad's okay now, isn't he?"

"Yes, thank goodness. But he still has to curtail his activities and watch his diet."

"Well, he's lucky to have you to help him. And you're lucky to have him," Laney said wistfully. "I remember how close you used to be. I always envied your relationship."

Laney's father had died when she was a young child, and a string of stepfathers followed. Emma had lost her mother at an early age, too, but rather than fill the void by remarrying, her father had devoted his life to raising his daughter.

He'd left his job as a driller with Corbett Enterprises, an oil exploration firm, to become the caretaker at the family estate so that he wouldn't have to travel. He'd made a cozy home for them in the tiny cottage at the edge of the Corbett estate and like in the old movie, Emma had grown up watching and admiring the Corbett family from afar and dreaming of a romance with Ash.

"We need to get together soon," Laney insisted. "We have a ton of stuff to catch up on."

"I'd like that," Emma said with a smile.

"Just give me a little more time to get settled. I'll call you."

"Promise?"

"Of course."

"Because if you don't, I'll call you," Laney said. "I still have your dad's number."

"I'm not at Dad's," Emma said quickly. "I'm living in the main house."

The living arrangement had been one of Wesley's strongest selling points for the job.

He told her that she would have her own suite of rooms with a private entrance. When his mother didn't need her, she'd be able to come and go as she pleased. She could use the pool, the tennis courts…whatever she wanted. The mansion would be her home.

Her home…but not quite as the way she'd dreamed it would be.

She took a pen and notepad from her purse. "Here. I'll give you my cell number." She scribbled the number, then offered the paper to Laney.

But the other woman's attention was caught by something behind Emma. She turned and saw several men standing beneath the pier.

"What are they doing?" Emma asked curiously.

"They must have caught something. Someone hauled in a shark the other day." Laney grabbed Emma's arm in excitement. "Let's go see what it is."

"I can't. If I don't get back soon, Helen will be upset."

"Oh, let the old biddy get her panties in a bunch just this once. It won't hurt her." Laney grinned. "Come on, let's go take a look."

Before Emma could refuse, Laney pulled her toward the pier. Climbing over the metal railing, the two women scrambled down the slight incline to the beach.

As Laney jumped down to the sand, she called out to one of the men. "Hey, Rick!"

Emma recognized Rick Bledsoe from high school. Her father had mentioned that he was now a deputy with the county sheriff's office, but he wasn't in uniform today. He had on shorts and sandals and looked as if he'd just come in from fishing. When he spotted Laney, he waved.

"What is it? Did someone catch another shark?" she asked.

Slowly he shook his head.

Laney started across the sand toward him, and he left the group to meet her halfway. He stood between Laney and the men, but Emma remained a few steps behind them and her view was unobstructed. In the gap left by Rick's departure, she saw a pale arm stretched out on the sand.

She came to an abrupt stop, her mouth going dry with dread.

Rick must have heard her gasp because he glanced at her before putting his hand on Laney's shoulder. "You don't want to go over there."

"Why not?" Laney tossed back her blond hair. "I've seen sharks before."

"It's not a shark." It was Emma who spoke instead of Rick.

Laney turned in confusion. "What is it then?"

Emma's gaze lifted to Rick's and he nodded, his expression grim. "It's a body," he said quietly.

"What?" Laney whirled back to face him, her hand flying to her mouth. "Oh, dear God. Who is it? Someone we know?"

He hesitated. "Hard to say. I'm not sure I've ever seen her before."

"Her?"

"It's a woman," he said, still in that hushed tone. "I know that much."

"Maybe I'd better have a look," Laney said.

"I don't think that's a good idea." Rick still

had his hand on Laney's shoulder and Emma saw something flicker in his eyes that chilled her blood.

"He's right," she said. "Maybe we'd better go."

But Laney remained adamant. "You two just chill. I'm a nurse, remember? I can handle it."

Rick shook his head. "You may be a nurse, but I doubt you've ever seen anything like this. Trust me on this one, Laney. You don't want to see that poor woman's face."

Chapter Two

One month later

"Your name is Ashton Corbett, but everyone calls you Ash. From this day forward, you need to get used to thinking of yourself as Ash. For all intents and purposes, Tom Black is dead."

The man who had been known as Tom Black until three days ago gave the seedy lawyer a look of contempt. "Aren't you jumping the gun? We haven't agreed on the money."

The lawyer's tone sharpened. "I take it that means you've decided to accept my offer providing we reach a satisfactory financial arrangement."

"I'm here, aren't I?"

"Yes, indeed you are. And the sooner we get started, the sooner this whole thing can play out to our mutual satisfaction." David Tobias all but rubbed his hands in glee. "First things first, though. As I said, from this moment forward, I will address you as Ash and you must start thinking of yourself accordingly. For this to work, you must *become* Ash Corbett. Not just pretend to be him. Do you understand the distinction?"

"My name is Ashton Corbett," he said in a monotone. "Ash for short."

The lawyer scowled. "Come now, say it like you mean it. Being a Corbett is something to be proud of. You're Ashton Corbett. Helen Corbett's grandson. That means something around these parts."

"I'll practice," he said dryly.

"You'll need to do more than practice. You'll have to live, breathe, sleep Ashton Corbett if we're to make this thing work."

"And just how do you plan for it to work?" he demanded. "You say I resemble Ash Corbett, but I can't look that much like him. Not enough to fool his own family."

"You're forgetting that he's been gone for twelve years. He was only eighteen when he left home, and before that, he'd spent years in boarding school. He was hardly ever around. Besides, some people's features change a great deal as they get older. And you've been through a lot. You were in a pretty bad car accident, right? You can always say you had plastic surgery."

"Wouldn't I have scars?"

"The wonders of modern medicine," the lawyer said with a shrug. "Stop borrowing trouble and trust me. I would never have involved myself in such a risky endeavor if I weren't absolutely certain it could work. You may not look exactly like the pictures I showed you of Ash, but you certainly resemble his father, at least enough to be related."

The imposter still wasn't convinced he could pull this off, but he said nothing as the lawyer rambled on.

"Nevertheless, we'll still have to play this very carefully because even though I was dumbfounded by the similarity when I first spotted you, I also noticed the differences. The way you look, the way you carry yourself...I knew almost instantly that you weren't Ash Corbett."

"But you went poking around in my background anyway, didn't you?"

The lawyer smiled. "I had to know for sure who I was dealing with before I made contact. And as for financial compensation, I mentioned before there's a sizeable inheritance from Ash's...excuse me...from your dead mother."

"How much?"

"A quarter of a million dollars. Now that you're over twenty-one, the money is yours free and clear."

"And the family will turn that kind of cash over to me just like that. No questions asked."

"They won't have a choice. Renata Corbett—Ash's mother—made the provisions before she took him back to Italy after her husband died. This money has nothing to do with the family."

Tobias swung his briefcase onto the desk in the shabby motel room and snapped open the locks. "The inheritance will be yours providing you adhere to the terms of our agreement. You must convince Helen Corbett that you're her grandson and that you have absolutely no interest in Corbett Enterprises. If you fail to do so within a reasonable amount of time, our agreement will be terminated."

The imposter went over and sat down on the bed. Catching a glimpse of himself in the mirror, he turned away. He didn't much like what he saw.

Pulling a pack of cigarettes from his shirt pocket, he grabbed the butane lighter on the nightstand and lit up.

Tobias whirled in distress. "Put that out!"

He squinted at the lawyer through a cloud of blue smoke. "Excuse me?"

"I said, put that out." Tobias walked over and snatched the cigarette from his fingers, then ground it out in the ashtray. "You don't smoke."

He gave a sharp laugh. "Like hell I don't."

"Ash Corbett doesn't smoke," the lawyer said slowly, as if trying to make his admonition sink in. "Understand?"

"How do you know I don't smoke?" the imposter asked in amusement. "You haven't seen me in years. I may have picked up a lot of bad habits you don't know about."

Tobias glared at him. "This isn't a joke, young man. It's in everyone's best interest for this to work out, but especially yours. With your record, you could be facing some serious jailtime if you don't pull this off. So I advise you to listen to what I have to say very carefully...*Ash*."

"Okay. Whatever. I don't smoke," he said lazily. "Anything else I'm not allowed to do?"

"We'll get into that later. But for now let me make something very clear to you. Once we start down this road, there'll be no turning back. If you have any questions or reservations, now is the time to voice them."

"I think you should be the one with reservations."

Tobias frowned. "Why do you say that?"

He got up from the bed and strode over to the window to glance out. "Say I do manage to convince the old broad—"

"Her name is Helen Corbett. She's your grandmother so show some respect."

He flashed a grin over his shoulder. "Say I manage to convince my *beloved grandmother* that I'm her long-lost grandson… why would I still need you around? What would keep me from going after the whole enchilada?"

Tobias's expression turned wary. "What do you mean by the whole enchilada?"

"I've done a little research since you showed up at the construction site the other day. Corbett Enterprises is worth a lot more than a quarter mil. They have oil leases all over Texas and Mexico. What makes you think I'll be happy with the money from my dead mother?"

"Because it's a quarter million more than you have right now," the lawyer snapped. "And likely a good deal more than you'd otherwise see in your lifetime."

He had a point there, the imposter thought.

Tobias picked up a folder and waved it in the air. "Don't forget, I've done my research, too. Tom Black doesn't have two nickels to rub together. He grew up dirt poor in Plaquemines Parish, Louisiana—lost both parents by the time he was twelve, in and out of foster homes until he turned eighteen, served a stint in the army and another in a state correctional facility, settled in New Orleans and tried his hand at construction until Katrina came along and wiped him out. He evacuated to Houston with thousands of others and from there he eventually moved to San Antonio and then here to Corpus Christi following work. Tom Black lives from paycheck to paycheck. Home is this rat-infested motel while he tries to save up enough money to get back on his feet. Ash Corbett has two hundred and fifty thousand dollars to do with as he pleases. He could go back to New Orleans...or disappear off the face of the earth."

"My, my. You have been busy, haven't you?" he said with an edge of rancor.

"Oh, there's more, but I think you get my point. You have a lot to gain from our collaboration, but if you try to claim any portion of the Corbett holdings other than the mother's inheritance, you will be exposed as an imposter and prosecuted to the fullest extent of the law. And if you think that you can take me down with you, think again." Something glinted in Tobias's beady little eyes. Greed, yes, but something else, too. A cruelty that he'd kept hidden until now.

It would be a mistake to underestimate him, the imposter thought. It would also be a mistake to think that he could walk away unscathed with the money. No scheme ever worked out the way it was planned. He'd learned that lesson the hard way.

He pulled down a slat in the blinds and stared out at the parking lot. Heat rose from the asphalt and shimmered like a mirage against a backdrop of drooping palm trees and a few scraggly oleanders. He could see his beat-up Chevy at the end of the lot, the most recent dent barely discernible in the rust and corrosion that had accelerated in the salt air.

The car needed a transmission overhaul, a muffler and a set of new tires. But the lawyer was right. Tom Black didn't have two nickels to rub together.

He let the blinds snap back into place as he turned. "Even if I do manage to fool this woman—my grandmother—you said she has two sons and a daughter. Someone is bound to demand a DNA test."

Tobias shrugged. "That won't be a problem."

The imposter sat down at the table and folded his arms. "How can it not be a problem? They can't be so gullible as to accept my word for who I am. I wouldn't."

The lawyer smiled. "Don't worry about that. Your appearance is different, but, as I said, we can explain that away. The resemblance is still quite striking, and after we're finished, you'll know things about Ash—about the family—that only he could know."

"You've thought of everything, haven't you?"

"As much as humanly possible, but even as thoroughly as we prepare, some will still have doubts. They've believed for years that Ash was dead and now for you to turn up out of the blue…" He paused. "One or both of the uncles will demand further proof… you're right about that. But it won't matter because we have a sample of the real Ash's DNA."

We?

Someone behind the scenes was pulling the strings; Tobias was just a puppet. And that someone needed Ash Corbett alive…for the moment.

A premonition of dread settled over him as he stared at the lawyer. "Do I want to know how you got the real Ash's DNA?"

Tobias grinned, displaying rows of perfect white teeth. "A few hairs from a comb, an old toothbrush. You don't need to worry how I came by the sample. Suffice it to say that when the time comes we'll simply substitute your DNA for Ash's."

"As easy as all that."

"Money makes anything possible because everyone has a price. You're living proof of that, aren't you?"

Anger tore through him. He clenched his fists at his sides, resisting the urge to toss the creepy little lawyer out on his ass. He wouldn't do that, though, because Tobias was right. He did have a price.

"There's one thing I don't understand," he said.

"Just one?"

He ignored the lawyer's sarcasm as he slowly got to his feet. "What are you getting out of all this?"

"I'm being handsomely compensated, I assure you."

"Who's paying you?"

The lawyer hesitated. "I'm not at liberty to say."

"But it has to be one of the uncles. Or Helen Corbett's daughter."

"As I said, I'm not at liberty to divulge my client's identity, but I wouldn't even if I could. You might give yourself away if you knew. It's better this way. You won't run the risk of letting down your guard with anyone. Now—" Tobias stuck the folder back in his briefcase and closed the lid "—any more questions?"

"Just one for now." He turned back to the window. "When do we start?"

"Immediately. I've already begun laying the groundwork for Ash's return, but you won't make an appearance at the mansion for at least another month. It'll take us that long to prepare."

The imposter reached for the cigarette pack in his pocket, then let his hand drop to his side. The sun bouncing off windshields was blinding. He squinted, trying to decide if he had the guts to go through with this or not.

But what choice did he have? If he walked away from David Tobias's offer, what kind of life would he have?

"What do you want me to do for now?"

"Pack your belongings and give notice at your job. We need to get you out of Corpus before someone else spots you. For the next few weeks you'll be staying in a cabin I've rented in the Hill Country. It's completely isolated. No phones, no television, nothing to distract you."

"What about the nightlife?" he quipped.

"Don't worry, you won't have time to get bored. I'll provide everything you need in order to immerse yourself in Ash Corbett's life. But no matter how hard we prepare, there're bound to be unforeseen complications. I hope you're good at improvisation, Mr. Black, because you'll have to be very quick on your feet. Helen Corbett is nobody's fool."

He turned from the window. "Were you talking to me? Because I don't know anyone named Black. My name is Ash Corbett."

The lawyer beamed. "I think this arrangement is going to work out just fine for everyone concerned."

Not everyone, the imposter thought grimly.

HE TOOK THE LAWYER'S ADVICE and began thinking of himself as Ash Corbett. It wasn't that hard to do because Tom Black was not someone he'd ever particularly admired.

In some ways shedding that persona was like lifting a heavy weight from his shoulders. Tom Black was a screwup, a two-bit con, a man who never seemed to catch a decent break.

But Ash Corbett was educated and well-bred, a rebellious hell-raiser who'd chucked a fortune to go off searching for his place in the world.

Ash Corbett was a man who would command respect wherever he went. Tom Black was invisible. Or he had been until he'd been spotted on a construction site by someone close to the Corbett family a few weeks ago.

His mind drifted back to that fortuitous day. He and a couple of other guys had been framing out beachfront condos when he first noticed the black Mercedes drive slowly past the site. The car made another appearance the next day and again on the following day.

For nearly a week, the car showed up at the same time and drove slowly past the site. He and the guys joked about it at first—one of them obviously had a rich admirer—but as the week wore on, uneasiness settled over the job site.

Just what the hell was going on? they began to wonder.

At the end of the week, another car appeared, this one a silver Jaguar that pulled to the side of the road just a few minutes before quitting time. Ash was the last one to leave that day because he'd had trouble getting his car started. As he worked under the hood, a man got out of the Jag and tentatively approached him.

"Ash? Ash Corbett? It is you, isn't it?"

He glanced over his shoulder as he continued to scrape away the corrosion from his battery posts. "Sorry. You've got the wrong guy, buddy."

"You're not Ashton Corbett?"

"Will it get me a jump if I say yes?"

"Forgive me," the man said with an apologetic smile. "I thought you were someone else."

"Yeah, I got that," he said dryly. "Now what about that jump?"

"Tell you what. I'll have my auto club come out and get your car started if you'll give me a few minutes of your time." When he hesitated, the man said, "I'll even throw in a new battery."

"Now why would you do that?"

"Because I have a kind soul," the man said,

but his smile was anything but pleasant. "I assure you, Mr. Black, if you'll give me a few minutes of your time, it will be worth your while."

A shiver of dread snaked up his spine as he straightened from the car. "How do you know who I am?"

The man beamed, obviously pleased with himself. "I think you'll find that I know a great deal about you, including the fact that you've done some prison time. Does your current employer know that you're an ex-con?"

He grabbed the man by his jacket lapels and shoved him up against the car. "Who the hell are you and what do you want from me?"

Fear flickered in the man's eyes, but he quickly got his emotions under control. "My name is David Tobias. I'm an attorney."

"An attorney?" he said with contempt. He dropped his hands from the man's coat. "I don't have much use for lawyers."

"No, I imagine you wouldn't after the raw deal you received from the State of Louisiana. The prosecution's evidence against you was circumstantial at best. Any competent defense attorney would have gotten you off, but you were unlucky enough to get saddled with Nevil Bates as your public defender.

"According to the records, he didn't even cross-examine any of the state's witnesses, nor did he object to the so-called evidence that was admitted against you. He sat there and watched an ambitious prosecutor and an overzealous judge railroad you, and now for the rest of your life you'll have to contend with the fact that you're a convicted felon. But if it's any consolation, Nevil Bates has since been disbarred."

He listened to the attorney all the way through his exposition and then turned back to work on the battery without comment.

"You've been down on your luck ever since you got out of prison, haven't you, Mr. Black?"

"Get lost," he said without looking up.

"I would go so far as to say the bad karma started on the day you were born to an alcoholic father and a drug-addicted mother. But your luck is about to change."

"Oh, yeah?" He slammed down the hood and wiped his hands on his grimy jeans. "And who are you? My fairy godmother?"

"In a manner of speaking." The lawyer's smile made his skin scrawl. "I'm here to offer you a great deal of money, young man. And all you have to do is pretend that Tom Black never existed."

That part of the job had been easy enough. Tom Black could stay dead for all he cared, but the rest of the con wasn't so easy to swallow.

Tobias was right. He'd been down on his luck for longer than he cared to remember and he'd done some things he wasn't proud of in order to get by. But deceiving the people who had genuinely cared about Ash Corbett was a new low even for him.

He was a lot of things, but he'd never deliberately set out to be cruel or cold-blooded. However, desperate times called for desperate measures.

He could do this, he told himself as he stared at his reflection in the mirror each morning. He could pull off this scam because, in some ways, he'd been preparing for it his whole life.

TRUE TO THE LAWYER'S WORD, the cabin where he'd been staying for the past two weeks was completely isolated. No telephones, no cable TV and cell phone service was spotty at best. He didn't have a vehicle, but David Tobias came to visit every other day to bring fresh supplies and to quiz him on his progress.

He'd been provided a mountain of documents and photographs to go through, as well as several home videos to scrutinize for facial expressions, mannerisms and any unusual tics. He'd changed his smile and learned to hold his head a certain way. Small things like that had altered his appearance dramatically. He started to look more like the pictures of Ash that Tobias had provided, and he also spent a lot of time practicing the voice he heard on the videos. By the end of the first month, the lawyer was impressed with his progress.

"We're nearing D-Day," Tobias said one evening as they sat out on the back deck watching the sun sink below the treetops. Squirrels rushed back and forth on leafy branches overhead while a rabbit nibbled at a bed of impatiens. In another hour or so when dusk was upon them, the deer would come out. Ash would sometimes sit in the dark for hours watching the wildlife and thinking about the con he was about to perpetuate on an unsuspecting family.

No matter how he justified his actions, when all was said and done, a lot of lives were going to be changed, maybe even destroyed if he wasn't careful.

"When do I make contact?"

Without answering, Tobias opened his

ever-present briefcase and took out a stack of photographs. "These are new," he said. "Go through them carefully and make sure you recognize everyone in all the shots."

He did as the lawyer told him, flinging each photograph onto the table as he recited names aloud.

"My Uncle Wesley and his wife, Pamela. My Uncle Brad and his wife, Lynette. Aunt Maris. Grandmother."

He continued through the pictures, which included more shots of the family, as well as the staff. He paused on a picture of a young woman who'd been caught in the same frame as the caretaker, Dominick Novick.

After studying the photograph for a moment, he passed it to Tobias. "Who is this woman?"

Tobias glanced at the picture, then tossed it onto the table with the rest. "That's Emma Novick. She's the caretaker's daughter. You've seen pictures of her," he said. "She may even have turned up in one or two of the home videos I gave you. I know I told you about her. She works for Helen now."

Ash reached for the picture, his brow furrowing as his gaze fastened on the young woman's face. "She looks different," he muttered.

"That's to be expected. She was just a

teenager when you left. Now she must be…
what? Nearly thirty, I would imagine."

He couldn't seem to tear his gaze away
from the picture. The woman had her head
turned away from the camera, and the way
she stood near the edge of the frame made
him wonder if she'd tried to take herself out
of the shot. He couldn't see her face clearly,
but he had the impression of sadness.

She was a far cry from the smiling girl
who'd been captured in the home videos
alongside Ash. Tobias had said the two of
them had been inseparable when Ash first
came to live with his grandmother, but as they
grew older, Helen had made sure that they
both knew their places.

She'd sent Ash to a boarding school up
north so that he could cultivate the right sort
of friendships, and when he was home during
holidays and summer, she filled his time with
lavish parties and glittering soirees.

According to Tobias, Ash had outgrown his
friendship with Emma, but she'd worn her
heart on her sleeve in those old home videos.
The way she gazed at him when she thought
no one was looking was a dead giveaway.

The video camera had captured a quietly
beautiful girl with long dark hair and wide,

soulful eyes. But as he stared at the woman she'd become, something akin to pity stirred inside him.

She'd had a difficult life. A bad divorce. A tragic love affair. Something had etched unhappiness deeply into the delicate curve of her back and shoulders. As he stared at the picture, he felt an unexpected connection with her, a bond that he couldn't deny.

He glanced up and found the lawyer's eyes on him.

Tobias said softly, "I know what you're thinking. But don't get any ideas."

"What are you talking about?"

"Emma Novick. She's still pretty enough, I suppose, but she's not the sort of woman that Ash Corbett would ever be attracted to."

"And you know this how?"

Tobias reached over and snatched the picture from his hand. "Don't complicate things. You need to put all your focus on Helen."

"Don't worry about me," the imposter said with a frown. "I know my part."

And God help him, he intended to see this thing through, no matter what it cost him.

Chapter Three

When Emma picked up the phone in her room that evening, she was taken by surprise to hear her employer's voice on the other end. Helen Corbett rarely sent for her once she'd been dismissed for the day, and it was even more unusual that she would ask Emma to come to her suite rather than to the downstairs study where they normally worked.

Emma had only been to the wing that housed Helen's private quarters once in the whole time she'd been living in the mansion and that was to deliver a package. Helen hadn't invited her in that day and she'd made it clear that once she retired upstairs, she was not to be disturbed for any reason.

That frosty admonition was still fresh in Emma's mind, and even though Helen had summoned her this time, she still felt a measure of trepidation as she knocked softly on the door before stepping inside.

Pausing just inside the doorway, Emma glanced around curiously. The first thing that struck her upon entering the suite was that the heavy ornate furniture and rich burgundy color scheme suited Helen.

The vaulted ceiling and stained-glass windows made the room seem stately and regal, while the sumptuous silk draperies and crystal chandelier provided a touch of opulence. The elegant, old-world décor reeked of refinement and tasteful indulgence—the kind that came from generations of wealth.

Emma was suddenly glad that she hadn't changed out of her navy suit. The jeans and sneakers she normally put on after work would have felt out of place in such luxurious accommodations.

She didn't have a clue why Helen wanted to see her so late in the day, but she wondered if it might have something to do with the visit earlier from David Tobias, Helen's lawyer. He'd come to the house right after lunch and Helen had sent Emma away because she needed to speak to him in private.

Emma had used the time to get some fresh

air. She'd been sitting in the garden reading when she heard David Tobias's car pull away from the house and head down the winding drive. She'd gone back inside to see if Helen wanted to finish the correspondence they'd been composing when the lawyer's visit interrupted them.

But the older woman had been too distracted to concentrate and instead had found fault with every little thing Emma did.

Finally, Helen had thrown her hands up in exasperation and left the study, muttering to herself about a certain person's incompetence. She'd gone straight upstairs and sequestered herself in her room until sending for Emma a few minutes ago.

"It's me, Mrs. Corbett. Emma." She closed the door and hurried across the thick carpeting of the sitting room to the arched doorway that led into the bedroom.

Helen's inner sanctum was airy and bright, less formal than the sitting room, but still elegant and lovely with its corner fireplace and floor-to-ceiling windows.

One of Helen's three-toed cats lay curled on the rug napping and twitching in a patch of dappled sunlight. Somehow the sight of the cat, so relaxed and unaffected by the grandeur of its surroundings, made Emma feel a little less intimidated.

"You wanted to see me?" she asked from the doorway.

The older woman was seated at her dressing table and Emma could smell her signature fragrance, an exotic blend of tuberose and lilies of the valley that was made for her by a famous perfumer in Paris.

Helen half turned on the stool. "I need your assistance, Emma. I sent Theresa away because she had the sniffles and God knows the last thing I need is to come down with a summer cold."

Theresa Ramon had been Helen's personal maid for as long as Emma could remember. She was getting on in years herself, but she still catered to her employer's every whim. And since the stroke, she'd become indispensable, though Helen would never admit.

"Of course, Mrs. Corbett, how can I help?"

"I'm having some difficulty with the clasp on this necklace. It's always been contrary." Helen's dexterity had been severely compromised by her illness, but she would never admit that, either. Far better to pretend that the jewelry was faulty.

"Here, let me see if I can get it to work."

Helen handed the necklace to Emma as she turned back to the dressing table and their gazes met in the mirror.

She looks different, Emma thought in surprise.

And then she realized why. Helen's blue eyes sparkled with excitement and the corners of her mouth twitched from time to time, as if she were harboring a secret.

Whatever news David Tobias had brought her obviously agreed with her now that she'd had time to digest it.

In spite of her age and health, Helen was still an attractive woman. She'd never been a great beauty, but she'd always had presence. A regal persona with more than a hint of mystery.

When Emma was little, she used to climb the oak tree that grew at the edge of the flagstone terrace and hide in the branches so that she could watch the lavish parties in the mansion. It was like having a glimpse into a magical world that she could hardly imagine.

The terrace would be aglow with tiny white lights in the shrubbery and candles set adrift in the spectacular pool. In the spring when the roses were out, the scent would fill the night air, along with the sweet aroma of lilies and camellias and hothouse-grown narcissuses.

In the summer, the more exotic fragrances of jasmine and plumeria would hang drowsy and seductive in the heat.

And in the center of it all, elegant and aloof Helen in her silks and diamonds. Always diamonds. The icy jewels fitted her perfectly—cold and hard on the outside, but with flashes of fire on the inside.

"Well?" Helen demanded. "Can you get it to work or not?"

"Sorry." Emma shook off the memories as she clicked the safety catch into place. The sparkle from the stones drew her gaze back to the older woman's reflection. "You look lovely tonight, Mrs. Corbett."

"You don't need to flatter me, Emma, I'm not delusional. Or blind. I can see my reflection with my own two eyes. I'm an old woman. My day has passed."

But in spite of her derisive tone, something hopeful seemed to linger in her blue eyes as she ran her fingers down the silky sleeve of her gown. "I suppose I may be a bit over-dressed for a family dinner, but it's a special occasion. I want to look my best tonight because I have an important announcement to make. I've instructed everyone to be here no later than eight."

An important announcement? Emma wondered what it might be.

She glanced at her watch. "It's almost eight now. And I was just on my way out. Shall I walk with you downstairs?"

It was a tricky business offering Helen assistance without seeming to. But Emma had learned the hard way that her employer had little patience for those who would try to mollycoddle her because of her age or health, and her pride would never allow her to ask for assistance even if she needed it.

"In a moment." Helen's eyes were still on Emma in the mirror, but the subtle excitement had turned coy. She fussed with her hair even though every curl was perfectly in place. "You must be curious about my announcement, Emma."

She hesitated, not certain how she should answer such a leading question. What did Helen want her to say?

"I assumed it was a family matter," she said with a slight shrug. Meaning it was none of her business.

Helen carefully blotted her lips on a tissue. "It is. But you'll find out soon enough. And I expect the news will surprise you as much as anyone."

Was she being fired? Emma wondered in sudden alarm.

Then in the next instant she chided herself for jumping to conclusions. Although Helen never complimented her work, Emma knew only too well that the older woman wouldn't hesitate to voice her displeasure if she found Emma's performance lacking.

Besides, her dismissal would hardly be cause for a formal announcement at a family dinner.

"You know that my lawyer came to see me today," Helen said.

Emma nodded. "Yes, of course."

"He brought me some news that was quite unexpected. I wasn't sure what to make of it at first. I didn't want to get my hopes up because I hardly dared believe it was true."

Emma was curious in spite of herself. "Good news, I take it."

"If it's true, it could be a miracle. The answer to all my prayers." Helen's hands trembled as she put the tissue to her mouth again, this time to quell a sudden tide of emotion.

Emma was shocked. She'd never seen her like this. The action was so unlike the stoic Helen. Even in the wake of a devastating stroke, her strength had never wavered.

"What is it?" she couldn't help asking.

The gleam in Helen's eyes was a hard, brilliant blue. She was emotional, yes, but the calculation was still there, too. She had something on her mind...something that involved Emma.

Her nerves tingled in warning as their gazes connected again in the mirror.

Helen's chin lifted imperiously. "David came to tell me that Ash is back."

For a split second, her words didn't register with Emma. And then when the name sank in, the realization hit her straight in the gut.

She had to struggle to school her own emotions. She had to remind herself quickly that Helen knew nothing of Emma's late-night trysts with Ash. She knew nothing of the whispered confessions, the heated caresses that Emma had shared with the woman's beloved grandson.

"Ash is back," she repeated numbly.

"That's what David came to tell me today."

"He's...here? In Jacob's Pass?"

"No, not yet. Apparently, he's in Corpus Christi. He contacted David a few days ago and asked to see me."

"A few days ago," Emma said in a shell-shocked voice. Ash had been in Corpus Christi a few days ago.

He was still there, just a few miles from her at that very moment....

"I don't understand," she said softly. "Why would he go see your lawyer instead of coming here?"

"He thought the shock might be too great for me. And given the circumstances surrounding his abrupt departure, I suppose he might also wonder about his welcome."

Emma was still having a hard time catching her breath. "Did Mr. Tobias say where he's been all this time?"

"Here and there, I gather." The glitter in Helen's eyes rivaled her diamonds. She didn't take her gaze off Emma even for a second. "He did some time in the army. Traveled around a great deal. I expect we'll have to get the full story from Ash."

Emma's mouth had gone so dry she was almost afraid to speak. But she knew that Helen expected a response and she couldn't let the knot in her throat or the sudden tremble at the backs of her knees give her away.

"I still can't believe it," she said, amazed that her voice could sound so normal when her mind raced with questions. "If he's alive and well, why did he never contact...you?" She had almost said *me*. Emma tried to gather as much of her poise as she could before continuing. If she valued her job, she had to be careful what she said to Helen. "Why weren't your detectives able to find him?"

Helen's mouth thinned. "There were no detectives."

"But I thought…"

"That I'd hired private detectives to track down my grandson?" She tossed the tissue aside. "Everyone assumed that's what I'd do. Ash may have thought so as well, but it was his decision to leave. I wasn't going to hunt him down like a criminal, nor was I of a mind to beg him to come back home."

So you let him walk out of our lives.

Emma could hardly believe what she was hearing. She'd always assumed that Helen had moved heaven and earth to bring Ash back home, which was why she could never understand how he'd been able to just disappear the way he had.

But Helen hadn't even tried to find him. She'd let him go without a word.

If only Emma had known the truth back then…

And just what would you have done?

What *could* she have done? She'd barely been seventeen when Ash left home. She wouldn't have had the resources to hire a private investigator herself, nor would she have known how to go about finding him on her own.

Emma had eventually convinced herself that Ash must have met with a tragic misfortune because there was no other possible explanation for his silence. The young man she'd known and loved would never have knowingly left her in limbo if he could have helped it.

But apparently that's exactly what he did do.

And now he was back.

Helen's voice broke into Emma's thoughts. "You don't approve of the way I handled the situation back then?"

The question stunned Emma. Why would Helen care what she thought?

She swallowed past the emotion gathering in her throat and shrugged. "It's really none of my business. I'm just surprised, that's all."

"But you and Ash were friends at one time. You must have wondered why he left. Or… did he tell you?" The question was subtle, but Emma heard a hint of accusation in Helen's tone.

She shook her head. "No, of course not."

"He never contacted you after he left home?"

Emma's stomach tightened in dread. What was Helen fishing for?

"I never heard a word from him," she said truthfully. "Why would you think that I had?"

"I didn't. Not really."

Helen frowned into the mirror and she suddenly looked every one of her seventy-nine years. Whatever decisions she'd made regarding Ash hadn't been without regrets.

Small consolation, Emma thought bitterly.

"Perhaps I should have handled things differently, but he was such a headstrong boy," Helen said. "So much like his father. Reese left home, too, you know. He came back, of course, as I knew he would, but he brought that woman into our lives."

The hatred that quivered in her voice was yet another shock to Emma. She'd never known that Helen harbored any animosity for Ash's mother.

When Emma was little, the staff would chatter freely around her because most of the time no one even noticed her. She usually managed to overhear the latest gossip regarding the Corbetts, but she couldn't remember any talk about a rift between Helen and Renata.

Emma barely remembered Ash's parents. They hadn't lived at the mansion with Helen, and as far as Emma knew, rarely even visited, although by the time Ash was born, his father was already in charge of Corbett Enterprises.

On the occasions when Reese did show up at the estate, he always came alone, but until now Emma hadn't realized the significance of his solitary visits. Obviously Helen hadn't approved of his wife.

Emma did have one fleeting memory of Renata Corbett. It came back to her now as Helen fretted with the diamond necklace. Emma had only been ten or eleven at the time and she'd been hiding in the oak tree during one of Helen's magnificent balls.

As she peered through the branches, she saw a dark-haired woman in a strapless blue evening gown run onto the terrace. Emma's breath had caught at the sight. The woman looked like a movie star or an exotic princess. Emma had never seen anyone so beautiful.

A few moments later, Reese Corbett had followed her out to the terrace and the two of them had gotten into an argument. Bits of that conversation came back to Emma and she wondered why she hadn't remembered it until now.

"We can't put her off forever, Renata," Reese had said. "She wants to see her grandson."

"That's why she invited me here tonight, isn't it? She's finally willing to accept me if it means she can get her clutches into my son. It will never happen, Reese. Not as long as I'm alive."

"He's my son, too, Renata."

"Not for long. I'm taking him back to Italy as soon as I can make the arrangements. If anyone tries to stop me, I'll go to the police."

"With what? Speculation? Gossip? No one will believe you."

"Are you willing to take that chance?"

"Renata, please. Just give me a little more time."

"We're running out of time. Can't you see that? The longer we stay here, the greater her influence over Ash. My mind is made up, Reese. I love you and I wish with all my heart that you would come away with us. But I'm very much afraid that you will never leave here again."

Neither of them said anything for a long time, and then Renata walked over and lifted her hand to caress his cheek.

"You're a good man, Reese. A decent man. You're not like the others. Always remember that."

"I'm a Corbett," he'd said bitterly, removing

her hand from his face. "Nothing will ever change that."

The memory drifted away and Helen's reflection wavered back into focus. She looked at Emma strangely, as if she somehow knew what she was thinking.

A shiver raced up Emma's spine. What did the memory mean? And why had she never thought of it until now? Maybe the hatred in Helen's tone when she spoke of her dead daughter-in-law had triggered it. Emma had forgotten the conversation because until now it meant nothing to her.

Obviously, there had been no love lost between Helen and Renata, and Emma couldn't help wondering why they'd disliked each other so intensely. Was it simply a case of an overbearing mother-in-law with too much control over her grown son's life?

Or had Renata another reason for despising Helen? She'd sounded almost afraid of her.

She's finally willing to accept me if it means she can get her clutches into my son. It will never happen, Reese. Not as long as I'm alive.

Emma's gaze darted away from Helen's reflection as a terrible thought seized her.

Not as long as I'm alive.

Don't, Emma warned herself. She would be foolish to make too much of conversation that she'd overheard nearly twenty years ago. For all she knew, her subconscious could have manufactured the memory, or at least part of it. She'd always had an active fantasy life, particularly when it came to the Corbetts.

Her gaze flickered back to Helen's. She was a moody, cantankerous, sometimes-cruel old woman, but she wasn't a murderer. No matter how much she'd hated and resented her son's wife, she would never have done anything to hurt her. She couldn't have had a part in Renata's death.

"Ash and I had a terrible argument the night he left home," Helen said. "He forced my hand. I couldn't send someone after him without seeming weak."

Emma wondered if the explanation was for her benefit or if Helen were trying to reassure herself that she'd done the right thing.

"What did you argue about?" she tried to ask without emotion. Without accusation.

Helen's rare moment of self-doubt vanished as obstinacy settled over her features. "The details are no one else's concern, but I had my reasons for letting him go. I knew that when the time came, he'd return to me—just as his father had before him—ready to assume the responsibilities of his heritage."

The responsibilities of his heritage.

The barrier that had always stood between them, Emma thought with a sudden stab of anger. Maybe that was why Renata had resented her, too.

Reese had been Helen's eldest son and he'd been groomed from childhood to take over the family holdings.

When he was killed in a car accident, his controlling interest in the company had reverted back to Helen to be held in trust for Ash, when and if she deemed him ready to assume the reins.

Something else came back to Emma now, something she hadn't thought about in years. A few weeks after Reese's funeral, Ash's mother had packed their bags and taken him back to Italy to live with her family. She'd overheard some of the staff talking about it, but if there'd been speculation at the time regarding her motives, Emma didn't remember it. They'd seemed to think it only natural that the young mother would want to be with her own family while she grieved.

But a few months later, tragedy struck again. Depressed and despondent over her husband's death, Renata took an overdose of sleeping pills one night and never woke up. Twelve-year-old Ash found himself once more uprooted from his home and brought back to live with his paternal grandmother, who had been awarded guardianship.

Emma could still remember the day that Ash arrived at the estate, a quiet adolescent with the saddest eyes she'd ever looked into. He hadn't spoken two words to her that day, had barely even acknowledged her presence. But for Emma, it had been love at first sight.

"And now he's back," she murmured.

"Yes," Helen said on a sigh. "He's come back home where he belongs. But David says I mustn't get my hopes up just yet."

Emma frowned. "Why not? He's seen Ash, hasn't he?"

"Yes. He's also done a preliminary investigation and so far his story checks out."

"His story?"

"Apparently his appearance has changed quite dramatically. He was in an accident and had to have some reconstructive surgery."

"What kind of accident?" Emma asked anxiously. *Was he badly hurt? Did he make a full recovery?*

"A car accident. He claims the surgery

altered his appearance, but David isn't completely convinced." Helen paused, her expression turning thoughtful. "Of course, as my attorney, he has to be cautious. If he were to bring an imposter into my home it would be the end of his career, to say the very least."

The notion had never even occurred to Emma.

An imposter. A man only claiming to be Ash.

That would certainly explain his silence all these years.

Emma didn't know whether the idea of an imposter made her feel better or worse. She wanted to believe that Ash was still alive and well somewhere, but the knowledge that he had been able to leave her so easily rankled, though she told herself she was a fool for still caring.

Whether he was an imposter or not, he wasn't the same man she'd fallen in love with. The same man who had held her so tenderly and kissed her so passionately that summer. What they'd shared had been nothing more than a teenage infatuation. A forbidden relationship elevated in importance by its very secrecy.

Emma drew a breath. "I don't see how anyone could pull off a scam like that with modern technology. All you have to do is have a DNA test performed."

Helen scoffed. "Now you sound like David. Do you really think that I won't know my own grandson? Twelve years won't have changed him that much. Ten minutes in the same room and I'll know if he's Ash."

It won't even take me that long.

All Emma had to do was look into his eyes.

Helen reached for her cane and struggled to stand. Emma knew better than to offer assistance. She waited until Helen was steady on her feet, then said, "I'll walk down with you. I'm on my way out to see Dad."

Helen nodded as she crossed the room. She was a few paces ahead of Emma and she turned to glance over her shoulder. "What I just told you isn't public knowledge yet. I don't want the news getting out until I've seen this young man for myself."

"I won't say anything. Not even to Dad."

"Thank you." Before she stepped into the hall, Helen paused again. "You must be wondering why I confided in you when I haven't even told the family yet."

"I'm sure you have your reasons," Emma murmured.

Helen's hand curled around the silver

head of her cane, and Emma saw her knuckles turn white as her grasp tightened. "I know at one time you fancied yourself in love with my grandson."

"Wh-what?" Emma stuttered in shock.

Helen gave her a disdainful look. "Please, Emma. Don't embarrass yourself or insult my intelligence by trying to deny it. I knew a great deal more about your relationship with Ash than you were aware. I didn't try to stop it because I knew he would grow out of his infatuation."

"I…don't know what to say," Emma managed to mutter.

"There's no need to say anything." Helen's mouth twisted cruelly and her eyes took on the intense gleam of blue steel. "I told you about my grandson's return as a kindness. I didn't want you hearing it from the staff or from someone in town. I thought you deserved that much."

"Thank you." But Emma knew that Helen hadn't told her of Ash's return out of kindness. She had another motive.

"Your father has been a diligent and devoted employee for many years and he would be the first to say that his loyalty has been amply rewarded. I would hate to think that anything would get in the way of that relationship, especially now that he's so close to retirement."

The threat was neither subtle nor frivolous. If Emma harbored any thoughts of picking back up where she and Ash had left off, Helen was prepared to resort to drastic measures. Her father would be fired, and at his age and with his health issues, new employment would be next to impossible to come by.

Anger heated Emma's cheeks and she found herself unable to respond for a moment for fear she'd say something she shouldn't.

Helen smiled. "You're a smart woman, Emma. I'm glad to see that you've learned a measure of restraint over the years."

Chapter Four

In spite of Helen's warning and the resulting tension between the two women, she clung to Emma's arm as they descended the stairs.

An elevator had been installed after her stroke, but once her mobility progressed beyond a wheelchair, she refused to use the lift. Nor would she move to more manageable quarters downstairs. She'd spent most of her adult life in the west wing upstairs, she insisted, and had no desire to relocate, no matter the advantages to the staff.

But her stubbornness could only carry her so far. By the time they reached the bottom of the stairs, her strength had visibly waned. The hand that clasped Emma's arm trembled from the exertion and her steps across the marble foyer were slow and measured.

When they reached the library, however, she rallied. It was amazing to watch her disguise the pain and exhaustion as her shoulders went back and her chin lifted in determination.

Except for the cane she used to support herself, no one would ever know she'd been completely debilitated the year before. Her courage was undeniable.

Emma hovered in the doorway for only a split second before she stepped back into the hallway. She'd planned to slip away once she saw Helen safely downstairs, but Wesley Corbett's deep voice stopped her.

"Emma! Don't run away! Come in and have a drink with us."

The last thing Emma wanted was to be drawn into a Corbett drama. She had no idea what the family's reaction would be to Helen's news nor did she much care at the moment. She needed time to analyze her own emotions.

"Thank you, but my father is expecting me for dinner."

"Surely one quick drink won't run you late. Come on in. I insist." Wesley stood at the fireplace, one arm propped casually on the mantel as he watched Emma from across the room.

He was dressed in a charcoal suit with a silver tie, and his dark hair was combed straight back from a wide, intelligent forehead.

His eyes were blue, like his mother's, with the same shrewd—occasionally taunting—gleam.

At fifty-five, he was an attractive, confident man with an easy smile and an approachable demeanor, but also like his mother, he had an air of mystery about him.

He made no move to help Helen into a nearby chair because, like Emma, he knew better.

His wife, Pamela, was seated on one of the white sofas that flanked the fireplace. She wore a green silk dress with thick gold chains coiled around both wrists and metallic high-heeled sandals.

The smile she flashed Emma was cordial, but her emerald eyes were scathing and dismissive. "Yes, do come in and join us, Emma. Perhaps you'd be so kind as to fetch Mother a glass of wine. Theresa seems to be indisposed this evening."

Wesley took control before the moment became awkward. "I'll do the honors," he said cheerfully. "Mother, the usual? Emma?"

"I really should be going—"

"Nonsense, I won't take no for an answer. I was hoping to run into you tonight." He busied himself at the bar. Light from the chandelier sparked off the Waterford stemware as he poured two glasses of wine. "I've been meaning to tell you how much we appreciate all your hard work," he said over his shoulder. "Mother says you've become indispensable around here."

"I never said anything of the kind," Helen declared but the look she shot Emma was surprisingly benign. She fingered her necklace. "You may as well come in and have a drink," she grumbled. "Wesley won't stop harping until you do."

Emma came uneasily into the room. She noticed then that Wesley's younger brother, Brad, and his wife, Lynette, were seated on the sofa opposite Pamela. They both murmured a polite greeting but Brad's expression, as usual, was anything but warm.

Settling into his early fifties, he had the faded looks of a man who had lived the good life for far too long without any of his older brother's discipline.

All those years, first in Reese's shadow and then in Wesley's, had undoubtedly taken a toll on his ego, Emma thought. From the little she remembered of Ash's father, he'd been a charismatic man with sultry good-looks and a sometimes brooding personality. An irresistible combination as Emma knew only too well.

Though not as handsome as Reese, Wesley had his own appeal. He possessed the kind of bigger-than-life personality that made everyone else, especially his younger brother, fade into the background.

Emma had always liked Wesley. She'd never understood why he'd been attracted to a cold, calculating woman like Pamela... other than the obvious, of course. She was stunningly beautiful and at least fifteen years his junior.

Like Pamela, Brad's wife was blond, a quiet pretty woman with a voluptuous figure that in bygone days would have turned heads, but by contemporary standards, would probably be considered overweight, especially in comparison to the pencil-thin Pamela.

She wore a simple black dress adorned with a single strand of pearls around her neck, and her shoes, while undoubtedly expensive, were low-heeled and sensible.

Lynette sat very close to Brad on the sofa, her hand entwined with his as though she were afraid he might wander away from her if she released him. The smile she gave Emma seemed genuine, if somewhat distracted.

Emma accepted the wineglass from

Wesley and wondered when she could politely escape.

"How much longer are you going to keep us in suspense about this big announcement?" Brad said to Helen. Emma thought his tone sounded a little condescending, but Helen seemed not to notice or take offense.

"I'd prefer to wait for Maris," she said.

"That could be a while. She's probably been held up at the hospital again."

"She does keep crazy hours, doesn't she?" Lynette flashed a glance at her husband as if looking for approval for her observation.

Helen's daughter was the youngest of her children and a doctor. Brilliant and beautiful, Maris Corbett had always been kind to Emma, but something about her seemed off, as if her pleasant demeanor didn't quite reflect the truth of her emotions.

"Did I hear my name?"

Everyone turned as she sailed into the room. She was a tall woman with the regal bearing of her mother and the easy smile of her older brother.

She'd obviously taken time to change before she came over. No lab coats or sensible shoes for her. The white dress she wore was sleek and form-fitting and her matching three-inch heels had been designed for attention rather than comfort.

"Sorry I'm late," she said as she hurried over to kiss Helen's cheek. "There was an emergency at the hospital. I couldn't get away."

"You aren't late," Helen said. "We're still having drinks."

Maris straightened and turned to Wesley. "Oh, good, you've made martinis, I see. I could use one after the day I've had."

"Coming right up."

Maris's gaze lit on Emma, and if she were surprised to see the hired help having cocktails with the family, she didn't show it. "Why, hello, Emma."

"Good evening, Dr. Corbett. It's nice to see you."

"Good to see you, too. How's your father doing these days?"

"He's well, thank you."

Maris gave her a mock stern expression. "Are you seeing to it that he watches his diet and gets enough exercise?"

"I'm doing my best. Actually, I was just on my way over to see him." Emma placed her wineglass on a nearby table, anxious to make her exit as quickly and gracefully as she could. "I should probably get going. He's expecting me."

"Well, be sure and give him my best," Maris said with a smile. "Tell him if he needs anything to give me a call."

"I will, thanks."

"Good night, Emma."

"Good night, Dr. Corbett." She nodded to the others and then hurried out before anyone, including Helen, could detain her.

Crossing the marble foyer, Emma slipped through the front parlor and out the French doors into the garden. Darkness had fallen, but there was still a bit of color in the western sky where the sun had disappeared below the horizon.

The estate was a quarter mile inland, yet Emma could smell the sea and a hint of rain in the warm breeze that blew in from the gulf. The moon was just rising over the treetops, a waxing orb half-hidden by the drift of wispy dark clouds.

The evening was soft and balmy. Crickets sang from the grounds, stirring memories for Emma.

As she moved along the flagstone path, her shoulder brushed a spray of jasmine and the explosion of tiny white stars released a heavenly aroma. She stopped and snapped off another sprig, then held the tiny white blossoms to her nose. The scent always reminded her of summer. And of…

Ash.

Ash.

A sigh trembled in her chest.

He was back. He was somewhere nearby at this very moment.

Emma tried to imagine what he might be like now, but all she could see when she closed her eyes was the way he'd looked the instant before he kissed her for the very first time.

His blue eyes had gone darkly intense as he lifted a hand to tuck a spray of jasmine into her hair. And then his fingers had slipped around the back of her neck and he pulled her to him. Emma's heart had pounded as he lowered his head to hers.

She'd turned seventeen that summer and had never been kissed. Not really kissed. Not the way Ash had kissed her that night.

He was only a year older, but already experienced. Already a player with his pick of girls who were much more beautiful and sophisticated than Emma. Girls who were more suited to his station in life. Girls his grandmother would approve of.

Once he'd been sent away to school and they'd stopped being friends, Emma had thought that he'd forgotten all about her. He seemed not to even know that she was alive.

But as she'd gazed up at him that night, she somehow knew that the flair of intimacy between them wasn't a fluke. Ash had wanted to kiss her for a long time. The longing was there in his eyes and in his voice when he murmured her name.

Emma.

She could almost hear his deep whisper in her ear, the feather of his lips along her neck, and she shivered at the memory.

More kisses had followed and the intimacy deepened. And by the end of the summer, Emma was head over heels in love. And Ash had felt the same way about her. She'd been sure of it.

But then he'd packed his bags one night and left home without a word to her or anyone else.

For days Emma had sat by the phone certain that he'd call but he never had. He didn't write to her, either, and after awhile, she'd put away all her mementoes—the spray of jasmine, the birthday necklace, the notes he'd left for her in the summerhouse—and somehow she'd picked up the pieces and gone on with her life.

But she'd never forgotten him. Never gotten over him.

And now he was back.

She released a long breath as she closed the lid firmly on her memory box. It didn't matter. Not anymore. What they had was dead and buried, and Emma would be a fool to still have hope. Not after all these years. Not after what he'd done.

She felt a nostalgic pull for what they'd had; she couldn't help that. But it didn't mean anything. She wouldn't let it. She couldn't afford to.

Tossing the jasmine aside, she turned and left the garden.

THE CARETAKER'S COTTAGE WHERE EMMA grew up was almost hidden by the ancient water oaks that lined the private drive. She avoided the winding lane and instead took a path that led straight through the trees to the cottage.

As she neared the house, she could smell the honeysuckle hedgerows that lined the nearby highway. Fireflies flitted through the bushes and the bats were out, swooping down from the treetops as their radar vectored in on the mosquitoes.

Perched near the entrance to the Corbett estate, the one-story cottage was made of Texas limestone and draped on the northern side with ivy. It, too, looked like something from a dream, with casement windows thrown open to catch the breeze and a wind chime tinkling softly on the covered front porch.

A light was on in the kitchen, and as Emma ran up the stone steps and opened the door, the aroma of chili and fresh-baked cornbread enveloped her like an old friend.

"Dad?"

"In here!"

She threaded her way through the modest furnishings in the living room to the large eat-in kitchen in the rear. In the nearly twenty-five years that her father had lived in the cottage, nothing much had changed.

The rugged pine cabinets and black barn door hinges were original to the house, as was the plank flooring. The old throw rug that had been strategically placed in front of the sink was faded from so many washings.

No matter how threadbare and rustic, the cottage still seemed like home to Emma and probably always would.

Her father stood in front of the old Magic Chef stove stirring the pot of chili. He was tall and still muscular with sparkling brown eyes and a thick, grizzled beard.

"Smells good," Emma said as she went over to the stove for a sample.

"Before you get on my case, it's vegetarian," he said.

"I'll have you know, I wasn't going to say a word." Emma cooled a spoon of chili, then took a small bite. "Umm, not bad."

"Not good, either. Leave out the meat, leave out the flavor," Dominick Novick said with a heavy sigh.

"Yes, but your heart will thank you for it." Emma patted his shoulder. "And so do I."

"Fetch the bowls and we're ready to eat," he said.

Emma went over to the cupboard and got down one bowl. "Would you mind too much if I take a rain check on dinner tonight, Dad? I'm really not very hungry. I think I'd like to just go for a walk and then turn in early."

"A walk?" Her father frowned as he motioned toward the open window. "It's dark out."

"I know, but I won't go far. Just down to the gate and back."

Worry glinted in her father's dark eyes as he studied her for a moment. "You aren't trying to prove something, are you, Emmy?"

The nickname took her straight back to her childhood. Emma shrugged at his question, but her eyes broke and she looked away. "I don't know what you mean."

But her father wasn't buying her denial. "You know what I'm talking about. These nighttime walks of yours…they don't have something to do with what happened in Dallas, do they?"

He'd always been just a little too perceptive when it came to reading Emma, which was why she had no intention of saying anything about Ash's return.

"I don't want to become a prisoner in my own home again," she said. "So, yeah, I guess maybe I am trying to prove something."

"That's crazy," he said sternly. "What happened wasn't your fault."

"I know that. But even after he was convicted, I let that animal take control of my life. I let him make me afraid of my own shadow. I don't want to live like that, Dad. Not anymore."

"And you think walking around by yourself in the dark is the answer?"

She shrugged. "Probably not. But it's what I have to do."

"I wish you'd give yourself a break," he grumbled. "What you went through would frighten anyone. You're plenty brave, Emmy. I've always been proud of your courage."

Tears sprang to her eyes. "I'm not brave. I wish I was, but I'm not." She mustered a quick smile. "Kind of ironic, isn't it? I moved back here to get away from the violence in the city and a week after I arrive another body gets fished out of the gulf."

Her father laid the wooden spoon aside and came over to where she stood by the table. "You don't need to worry about that. It's a terrible thing, but it doesn't have anything to do with that filthy business twelve years ago. The sheriff's already made an arrest. The woman's husband has all but confessed."

"I know." By all indications, the poor woman that she and Laney Carroway had seen on the beach over two months ago had been a victim of domestic abuse. The murder didn't have anything to do with the bodies that had been found on Shell Island twelve years ago. It certainly didn't have anything to do with Emma's return to Jacob's Pass.

She gave her father a peck on the cheek, then tugged on his beard and said lightly, "You're right. That creep is behind bars where he belongs so stop worrying about me. I won't even leave the grounds."

He didn't question whether she was talking about the husband who had murdered his wife or the stranger who had broken into Emma's Dallas apartment and assaulted her. All he said was, "You've got your cell phone?"

"Right here." She patted her jacket pocket. "If I need you I'll call you."

She left him staring after her at the front door. At the end of the walkway, she turned and gave a quick wave, then headed up the winding drive that led to the main house.

Emma tried not to hurry. She tried not to keep glancing over her shoulder as she reminded herself that she was out for an evening stroll. There was nothing to be afraid of.

But the memories closed in on her and the hoot of an owl somewhere in the trees lifted gooseflesh on her arms. Her heart started to pound against her chest.

He's in jail. He can't hurt you. There's nothing to be afraid of anymore.

She repeated the mantra over and over as

she walked along in the dark. The man who had followed her home from work one night and pushed his way into her apartment had been apprehended fleeing the scene. Emma had picked him out of a lineup and then she'd testified against him at his trial. He'd been sent away for a very long time.

And you were lucky, she reminded herself. He hadn't had time to rape her as he had the other two women who had come forward. But he would have if a neighbor hadn't seen him enter Emma's apartment and called the police.

The assailant had held a knife to her throat as he ripped open her blouse and shoved up her skirt. Paralyzed with fear, Emma hadn't been able to fight him off. And that was what haunted her more than anything else. She'd been willing to submit rather than fight for her life.

She fingered the scar on her neck where he had cut her. *Make one sound and I'll slit your throat.*

She'd done what she had to in order to survive, the counselor at the rape crisis center had told her. The man was obviously willing to use the knife. Emma couldn't blame herself for what had happened. The attack wasn't her fault.

And deep down, she knew that. She hadn't invited a stranger into her home and she'd certainly done nothing to provoke him. He'd singled her out because he liked her hair, he told her. So the very next day, Emma had cut it all off. She'd changed the locks on her front door and varied the routes she used to and from work. She'd done everything in her power to protect herself...except fight off her attacker.

Emma was so caught up in the memories that she failed to hear the approaching car until it was too late. She turned just as headlights rounded a sharp curve in the lane and headed straight toward her.

The glare froze her for a split second before she lunged out of the way. Her foot slipped on a rock and she landed with a hard thud on her bottom. The misstep saved her because when she hit the ground she rolled a few feet down into a shallow ditch carpeted with dried pine needles.

The driver hit the brakes and the car came to a stop as a shower of gravel pelted the road like buckshot. The door opened and slammed, and then a voice said anxiously from the dark, "Are you okay? Did I hit you?"

The headlights were still on, but from where Emma lay she could only see his silhouette. She rose shakily to her knees, trying to determine whether or not she was hurt. When she decided she wasn't, she sprang to her feet in anger. "Are you crazy driving like that? You could have killed me!"

"I didn't expect anyone to be standing in the middle of the road after dark," he said defensively. "And dressed all in black, at that."

Emma brushed off her skirt. "It's navy. And I wasn't standing, I was walking."

"You were still in the middle of the road."

"For your information, this is a private drive. I have every right to be in the middle of the road…or anywhere else I choose."

"So do I."

The subtle, imperious tone stopped Emma cold and her breath seemed to hover somewhere in her throat.

He'd sounded so different at first that she hadn't recognized his voice. He looked taller than she remembered, too.

"Ash." She said his name before she could stop herself and she heard him inhale sharply.

Then he gave a little laugh. "I was wondering if you'd recognize me."

She moved toward him then, barely aware of the hitch in the ankle she'd just twisted. He still stood beside the car and when he moved his head, she got a better look at him in the glow of the headlights.

David Tobias was right, she thought. The years and the accident had changed him.

His mouth was the same, though, and his eyes...she wished she could see them better. The way he held his head made it impossible for Emma to look directly into his gaze.

"You look different," he said, taking the words right out of her mouth.

"Do I?" She fingered the razored strands of hair at her nape. "It's been a long time."

"Yeah, it has."

Was that regret she heard in his voice? Or was she merely projecting her own emotions on to Ash?

Awareness fluttered like a whisper along her nerve endings.

"You don't seem surprised to see me." He cocked his head and suddenly he looked exactly the way Emma remembered him.

Tears sprang to her eyes and she had to take a moment to compose her emotions. It was just a memory, she told herself. A brief glimpse into the past. Ash *was* different. He wasn't the same person he'd been twelve years ago and neither was she.

"Your grandmother told me you were

back." Emma was relieved that her voice sounded so normal. A little breathless, perhaps, but she doubted Ash even noticed. "She's not expecting you tonight, though."

He shrugged. "I didn't feel like waiting. Besides, there's nothing like catching someone by surprise to find out how they really feel about you."

"You don't think she'll be thrilled to see you?" Emma asked. "You were always her favorite."

"I'm not so much worried about her as I am...certain others."

Emma's heart started to pound in agitation. She moistened her lips as she stared up at him in the dark. "Like who?"

He leaned against the car and folded his arms. "When you take off the way I did, you leave a lot of unfinished business behind."

"Yes, I suppose that's true." Emma was suddenly at a loss. She'd imagined this moment for so many years, had even rehearsed in her mind what she would say to him.

How could you walk away from what we had?

Why did you let me think all these years that you were dead? How could you be so cruel?

Did you ever really love me?

As all the old questions flitted through her head, she suddenly realized that the time for asking them was long past. It didn't matter anymore. And that was why there was nothing left for them to say to each other.

"I like your hair."

The compliment took her by surprise and she laughed awkwardly. "Really? You used to like it long. You once made me promise to never cut it."

"A promise you broke, I see."

Regret tightened her chest. Not because she and Ash were nothing more than strangers to each other now, but for all the wasted years. For all the lonely nights she'd spent dreaming about a man that had apparently died the night he left home.

"I don't want to keep you," she said. "You're probably anxious to see your family. They're all at the house, by the way."

He grimaced. "All of them?"

"Your grandmother called a family dinner after she found out that you were back."

"Great," he said dryly. "I'd liked to have been a fly on the wall when my uncles heard that the prodigal nephew has returned to stake his claim."

"Is that why you came back?" Emma

couldn't help asking. "To stake your claim in Corbett Enterprises?"

"I came back because I was tired of running."

His response surprised her. "Running from what?"

A long hesitation, then he lifted a hand and rubbed the back of his neck. "Running from responsibility and familial obligations, I guess. Isn't that why spoiled heirs always run away?" The bitterness in his voice surprised Emma yet again. Ash had been a lot of things back then, but never bitter, not even in the aftermath of his parents' tragic deaths.

She suddenly wondered what he'd been through these past twelve years. What his life had been like. Helen had said he'd spent some time in the army, and Emma could see the hint of a soldier in the way he carried himself. Even reclined against his car, arms folded, ankles crossed, there was something about his demeanor that was watchful and wary.

"I won't keep you," she said again, anxious for this first meeting to be over and done with. Anxious to be alone so she could try and make sense of her own life. She'd come back to Jacob's Pass to heal and to remember, but now seeing Ash, seeing only a shadow of the man she'd once loved, Emma knew that it was time for her to forget.

"Are you on our way up to the house?" he asked.

"Yes. I…live there now. I work for your grandmother."

"So I heard. Hop in. I'll give you a ride back."

"Thanks, but I'd like to finish my walk."

"Are you sure? It's the least I can do, considering."

Considering what? Emma wondered. Considering he'd almost run her down or considering he'd once broken her heart.

She shook her head. "It's nice out. I'd rather walk."

For a moment, it seemed as if he might try to change her mind, but then he shrugged. "Suit yourself." He straightened from the car, his gaze still on her in the dark. "I guess I'll see you around then."

"Yes, I'm sure you will."

If his meeting with Helen went well, he'd probably move into the mansion. He and Emma would be running into each on a daily basis.

Not that it mattered anymore, she told herself again as she watched the taillights of his car fade in the distance.

Chapter Five

He watched in the rearview mirror until she was out of sight. His heart wouldn't stop pounding and his palms were so sweaty that he had to tighten his grip on the steering wheel.

Relax. It's over. You did okay.

Okay, but not great.

At least the first meeting was out of the way. Maybe he hadn't handled it as well as he should have, but each time would get easier.

At least he hoped so because at this rate, he wasn't sure he'd hold up under the pressure.

Now on to the next hurdle.

But before he faced the family, he somehow had to get a better grip on his nerves. Because once he stepped inside the mansion, he wouldn't have darkness to shield him.

He expelled a long, shaky breath. The worst was over. At least he was a little better prepared now. Seeing Emma Novick so unexpectedly that way—in the middle of the road, no less—had taken him by surprise. He'd damn near run her down so it was only natural that he'd been thrown off his game.

Plus, she looked different than she had in the photograph David Tobias had shown him the other day. Obviously the camera had caught her at an unflattering angle, because in person she looked much more like the girl from the old home videos he'd been watching for weeks.

Maybe the darkness had shielded her, too. Maybe it had softened her features, but he didn't think that was the case. He didn't think the darkness had anything to do with the impact Emma Novick had had on him.

"Forget it," he muttered, frowning at the road in concentration. David Tobias was right. He wasn't here to start something up with Emma Novick. He had to get his head on straight—and keep in that way—before walking into that house and looking Helen Corbett in the eyes.

If he'd known everyone would be present tonight he might have thought twice about showing up unexpectedly. Tobias would hit the roof when he found out. The first meeting with Helen Corbett had been carefully planned, but arriving unexpectedly and unannounced seemed the kind of thing Ash Corbett would do.

So here he was. Improvising. Exactly what Tobias had told him to do.

He stopped the car at the edge of the drive and let his gaze drift over the palatial estate. The sprawling house with its towers and domes reminded him of one of the old limestone and granite Victorian mansions along Broadway Street in Galveston.

The place was huge, but he wasn't worried about finding his way around. He knew the layout of the house by heart. David Tobias had made sure of that, even supplying him with a copy of the original blueprints.

"Your room is on the third story," Tobias had said using his index finger to trace a trail through the maze of hallways and hidden staircases. "You chose it when you first came to live with your grandmother because there's a view of the gulf from the east windows."

As the memory drifted away, he sat drumming his fingers on the steering wheel. Should he enter through the main hall?

According to Tobias, the family usually parked under the portiere at the side and came in through the garden doors, but Ash had been gone for a long time and his welcome was anything but assured. Showing up here unexpectedly was one thing, but walking in through the side entrance, as if he owned the place, was another.

No point in getting off on the wrong foot, he decided. Ringing the front bell and waiting to be escorted inside would show respect and a certain amount of contrition and uncertainty that Helen Corbett would probably appreciate.

Three cars were parked under the portiere. Tobias had mentioned that Wesley drove a white BMW and the beige Lexus belonged to Maris. That left the Lincoln Navigator for Brad and his wife, Lynette.

So who had been in the black Mercedes that had driven past the job site day after day? he wondered.

Pulling around the circular driveway, he parked in front of the house and got out of the vintage Mustang that Tobias had bought for him.

Nothing too fancy, the lawyer had explained. Ash hadn't exactly been leading a luxurious life since he left home, but the rusted heap he'd been driving wouldn't do, either. If he appeared too down on his luck he might arouse suspicion.

David Tobias had thought of everything. Or so he claimed.

Standing in front of the massive front doors, he glanced back at the car before ringing the bell. His bags were in the trunk. He wondered if he would need them tonight.

It was entirely possible that the lawyer had misjudged the whole situation. Helen Corbett just might send her errant grandson away without bothering to hear his carefully crafted story.

Here goes nothing.

Drawing a quick breath, he pressed his thumb to the bell and a few seconds later, the door was opened by a young woman wearing a black-and-white uniform.

"May I help you?" she said as she gave him a curious perusal.

"I'm here to see Mrs. Corbett. Helen Corbett."

Her expression was mildly disapproving as her gaze flicked over his casual attire. He wore jeans and a soft pullover shirt that he and Tobias had ordered over the Internet from a department store. He'd been given a whole new wardrobe so he guessed that no matter what happened with Helen, he'd at least come out of this deal better dressed.

"Is Mrs. Corbett expecting you?"

"Yes, but not tonight. Could you please tell her that her grandson is here to see her?"

Shock registered on the woman's pleasant face a split second before her training kicked in. She stepped back from the door. "Please come in. Mrs. Corbett is having dinner, but I'll inform her that you're here. You can wait for her in the library."

The moment he stepped through the door, he was enveloped by the grandeur of the foyer. His gaze lifted to the crystal chandelier suspended from the ceiling, then traveled up the ornate curving staircase to a second-story gallery where ancestral portraits hung on the walls.

A large arrangement of lilies and roses had been placed on a gilded pedestal at the foot of the stairs. The cloying scent made him think of a funeral he'd gone to as a kid. He hadn't liked the smell of hothouse flowers since then.

As he followed the maid across the pink-and-gray granite floor, he tried not to give away his curiosity by gazing around. Instead, he kept his eyes straight ahead as the young woman led him down a wide, paneled hallway and slid back the pocket doors to the library.

Her shoes were rubber-soled, he noticed. They barely made a sound on the hard surface as she stepped aside for him to enter.

"Mrs. Corbett will be with you shortly."

"Thanks."

She gave him another curious look before sliding the doors closed behind him. And suddenly he was alone again.

As he walked over to examine the crowded bookshelves, something else David Tobias said came back to him.

"The library is where Helen always receives guests and entertains family," Tobias had told him. "She and her husband—your grandfather—collected rare books. It was a shared passion and perhaps she still feels close to him in that room, although she's never been overly sentimental. At least not on the surface."

He ran his finger along the leather spines as he studied the titles. When he spotted a copy of *Robinson Crusoe,* he couldn't help smiling. He remembered enjoying that book as a kid. He'd like reading well enough, but where he went to school, it wasn't always cool to admit it.

He was still thumbing through the pages, admiring the illustrations, when he heard someone come into the room. He had his back to the entrance and didn't look up as the doors slid open, but his heart slammed against his chest.

This is it.

The moment that would either make him or break him.

Calmly shelving the book, he turned.

He'd braced himself to come face-to-face with the cold, haughty matriarch of the family, but the woman who stood glaring at him from across the room was much younger than Helen Corbett.

She was in her late forties, tall, attractive, with shoulder-length blond hair and eyes as piercing as a knife blade. Slowly, she walked toward him, her gaze never leaving his face.

"So it is you," she said softly, but her voice was edged with displeasure. "I could hardly believe it when Mother told us you were back. And then when Lucia said you were waiting for us in the library, I had to come and see for myself."

She walked up to him. She was a tall woman and the high heels she wore put her at eye level with him. That close, it was impossible not to see the anger tightening the corners of her mouth.

He gave her a tentative smile. "Hello, Aunt Maris."

The anger flashed in her eyes and she lifted her chin. "Don't 'hello, Aunt Maris' me, as if you've just been away for a week or two. You've got a lot of explaining to do, kid."

And then suddenly the anger disappeared and she was smiling ruefully, shaking her head. "I still can't believe it's you."

"In the flesh." He didn't quite know what to say so he let her take the lead.

"Well? Don't I at least get a hug?"

"Sure." He wrapped his arms awkwardly around her thin frame and held her for a moment before drawing back. But she would have none of that. She tightened the hug and kissed his cheek before letting him go.

Stepping back, she frowned. "Something's different about you."

"Well, it has been twelve years. I'm not a kid anymore."

"That's true. You're a grown man responsible for your own actions." She peered at him closely, as if trying to detect the scars from his surgery. Or maybe she was searching for internal scars. "You've a lot to account for, Ash. I wasn't kidding about that. Mother will want some answers. I hope you have some that will satisfy her, but somehow I doubt that you do."

He shrugged. "All I have is the truth."

"Well, that's a start, I guess." Maris smiled and patted his arm. "Don't look so worried. It'll be okay. She's so happy to have you home that she'll accept almost anything you tell her. Although she'd never admit it, of course. You'll need to do a bit of groveling just so she can save face."

"I was never all that good at groveling, but I'll see what I can do."

She laughed at that. "No Corbett worth his salt is any good at groveling, but you were even more headstrong that the rest of us. I'm guessing that hasn't changed."

He merely grinned.

They shared a moment of amusement, then her expression sobered. "I don't know what happened the night you left here, Ash. Mother would never talk about it, but I know you two had a terrible falling out. That's all water under the bridge now. Don't let your pride stand in the way of a reconciliation. Your homecoming could do her a world of good." She paused. "She had a stroke last year. It very nearly killed her. It would have anyone else."

He nodded. "I know about that. David Tobias told me."

"Then you must also know that her recovery hasn't been easy. I don't want to see her hurt again. I'm not sure she could take it."

"I didn't come back to cause trouble," he said. Then added, "For anyone."

She sighed. "You're talking about Wesley and Brad now, I suppose. Since Mother's stroke, she's turned the company over to Wesley. Brad is his second in command. They won't relinquish the reins willingly so tread carefully, kid."

"Like I said, I didn't come back here to cause trouble. Whatever claim I had to Corbett Enterprises was forfeited the night I packed my bags and left home. I understand that."

Maris frowned. "Let's not go overboard with the self-flagellation. My brothers could stand a little competition, especially Wesley. He acts as if Corbett Enterprises is his already, but so far as I know, Mother has never changed her will. As Reese's son, you're first in line to inherit controlling interest upon her death. Sooner, if she decides you're ready. When and if that happens, be prepared for a fight, Ash. And in the meantime, watch your back."

Before he could respond, voices from the hallway silenced them both and Maris quickly positioned herself at his side as the others came into the room.

Helen Corbett entered first, her bearing so straight and her steps so steady that if not for the silver-headed cane in her right hand, he would never have guessed that her health was so fragile.

As her gaze came to rest on Ash, something sparked in her blue eyes, but she wasn't smiling. Nor did her rigid demeanor invite his approach.

He remained where he was as the others— Brad, Lynette and Pamela—filed into the room behind her. Wesley came last, a tall, masculine version of Maris. There was warmth in his face and maybe even a hint of a smile, but the moment he saw Ash, his mouth thinned and his eyes went ice cold.

Maris squeezed his hand and said in his ear, "Just remember, I'm on your side. I always have been."

Then she slipped away and left him alone to face the lions.

ASH'S CAR WAS PARKED IN the circle drive in front of the house when Emma got back from her walk. He hadn't pulled under the portiere as everyone else had, and she wondered if that had been deliberate on his part or an unconscious way of letting everyone know that he no longer considered himself part of the family.

Or maybe he simply hadn't wanted to presume too much. Helen had always adored Ash, the only offspring of her favorite son, but she was also a tough old bird who wouldn't forgive or forget too easily. No matter how glad she was to see Ash, she wouldn't let him off easily. Not until he'd sufficiently repented.

For a moment, Emma stood staring at the car. It was a far cry from the Porsche Helen had bought him for his sixteenth birthday, and Emma was hard-pressed to imagine Ash Corbett as an ordinary guy, someone who worked for a living and worried about his bills.

She couldn't help wondering if his car— painstakingly restored—was a reflection of the man he'd become rather than the one he'd left behind.

Walking through the portiere, she let herself in through the garden gate. She'd meant to slip inside the house and hurry up the back staircase before she was seen, but someone stood smoking in the garden. When Emma saw who it was, she started to retreat through the gate, but the squeaky hinges had already signaled her presence.

"Hello, Emma." Pamela Corbett tossed her cigarette to the grass and ground it out with her foot. "Did you have a nice dinner with your father?"

Emma didn't bother correcting the assumption. Instead she smiled and said, "Yes, thank you."

"You weren't gone long. Did you just walk up from the road?"

"Yes."

The landscaping lights tucked into the lush shrubbery cast a subtle glow over the garden. Emma could still smell the jasmine and now the more woodsy fragrance of the moonflowers that spilled over the stone wall and tangled with the morning glories.

Pamela's face looked like porcelain in the light. She was a cool, beautiful blonde who seemed about as approachable as a cobra.

"You must have seen him drive up then."

"Who?"

She gave a low laugh. "Don't be coy. You know exactly who I'm talking about. Did you talk to him?" Her expression never changed, but Emma heard an anxious note in her sultry voice.

"You mean Ash? I spoke with him briefly. He almost ran me down on the road."

"Did he?" She laughed again. "Well, that sounds like the old Ash, doesn't it?" She took another cigarette from her bag and lit up. "What did you think of him?"

Like Helen earlier, she was fishing for something, but Emma wasn't about to bite. She said carefully, "As I said, I only saw him for a few moments."

"But you talked to him, right?" Pamela took a deep pull on the cigarette and blew out the smoke. "What did he say?"

"Nothing much. He wanted to make sure I was okay."

"After he almost ran you down." She smiled through the smoke. "That sounds like him, too. Careless...but unfailingly polite. That's our Ash."

Emma shivered at the venom in Pamela's voice. What had Ash ever done to warrant such contempt? "If you'll excuse me, I was just on my way to my room."

"Without saying good-night to Helen?"

"I don't want to interrupt her. I'll see her in the morning. Good night, Mrs. Corbett."

Emma started toward the French doors, but as she moved passed the fountain, Pamela caught her arm. Her eyes glittered in the darkness. "I know about you and Ash."

Emma's heart thudded against her chest as she pulled away.

"Oh, yes. I know all about it," Pamela said smugly. "The looks, the smiles, the secret rendezvous in the summerhouse. I suppose you were too young to realize what a cliché that was. Or maybe you just didn't care. Maybe you thought you'd be the exception and end up with your very own Prince Charming."

Emma moistened her lips. This was certainly a night for revelations. "How did you—"

Pamela shrugged. "I saw you slipping through the woods one night. I was bored so I decided to follow you. Ash was waiting for you in the gazebo and it was obvious the two of you were a bit closer than friends. But don't worry," she said, flicking her ashes into the fountain. "I never said anything to Helen or to Wesley. Your secret was safe with me. It still is…for as long as I have your cooperation."

Emma's blood turned cold at the thought of conspiring, on any level, with the likes of Pamela Corbett. "I don't understand. What is it you want from me?"

"It's really quite simple. I want you to be my eyes and ears while you're in this house."

"What do you mean?"

"You're a clever girl, Emma. You know exactly what I mean. I saw Ash a few minutes ago. He's very different from the young man who left here twelve years ago. You must have noticed that, too."

Emma tried to keep her voice even. She didn't want Pamela to see her apprehension because she knew the woman would somehow try to use it against her. "As I said, we only spoke for a moment and it was dark. I really didn't get a good look at him."

"I'm not just talking about his appearance, although if you ask me he's lost his looks." Pamela propped her elbow on her arm as the cigarette smoldered between her fingers. "He's older, harder…he's not the same person he was twelve years ago."

"None of us are," Emma said.

"No, that's true. But I have a hard time believing that someone could change as much as he has. Even if he did have an accident and reconstructive surgery, that doesn't explain why he never called or wrote the whole time he was gone. I understand that he left in anger, but twelve years is a long time to hold a grudge. I'm curious about his timing, aren't you?"

Emma said slowly, "You don't think he is Ash, do you?"

Pamela moved away from the fountain and came toward Emma, a stream of smoke trailing her in the dark. The pungent aroma mingled with her perfume and the sweeter scent of the flowers in the garden. "What do you think, Emma?"

"I have no reason to believe he isn't who he says he is."

"Maybe not yet." Pamela's gaze burned into hers. "But you're in a very unique position. If anyone can determine whether or not the man inside that house is an imposter, it's you."

"How?"

She clucked her tongue in disgust. "You're still being deliberately dense. I'm disappointed in you."

"Mrs. Corbett—"

"Get him alone, Emma. Do what comes naturally."

Emma's cheeks heated with anger. "You're asking me to seduce him and then tell you whether or not I think he's an imposter? That hardly falls under my job description."

"Oh, crawl down off that high horse,"

Pamela said scathingly. "It's not like you haven't seduced him before. You were shameless the way you used to chase after him so please spare me your moral superiority. Besides, I'm not asking you to sleep with him. Unless you want to, of course. Just get him alone. The two of you must have shared secrets."

First Helen had warned her away from Ash, and now Pamela was trying to get her to seduce him. Emma suddenly felt trapped between two very dangerous predators and she knew she had to tread carefully. Her father's livelihood and her own depended on it.

"I'm sorry, Mrs. Corbett, but whether the man inside that house is an imposter or not is none of my business. Whoever he is, he's a stranger to me and I intend to keep it that way. Besides, Helen will surely order a DNA test."

"I'm sure she will, but that could take weeks. In the meantime, a clever con man— as I suspect he is—could do a lot of damage to this family. What if he ingratiates himself with Helen and then she learns he's not her beloved Ash? Do you think she could take a shock like that?"

Pamela's concern for her mother-in-law rang hollow. She had something else up her sleeve, and whatever it was, Emma wanted no part of it.

"You're not giving Mrs. Corbett enough credit," she said. "She's a very shrewd woman. If he's an imposter, she'll see right through him. She doesn't need me for that."

"Helen's smart, I'll grant you that. But she's been through a lot this past year and her mind isn't as sharp as it once was. Besides, she adored Ash. She even put him ahead of her own sons. She's going to desperately want to believe that man is her grandson."

"I still think you're selling her short," Emma said.

"I hope you're right. But I think Helen will believe just about anything if it means she can have her precious Ash back." Pamela's tone turned bitter. "He's still her heir, you know. She hasn't changed her will in all these years. Even after everything Wesley has done for the company."

So that was it. It all came down to the money.

Emma wasn't surprised. Pamela Corbett had always struck her as the mercenary type. Naturally she would have her own best interests at heart, probably more so than her husband's.

"If you don't want to do it for me, then do

it for Wesley," Pamela coaxed. "After all, he went out of his way to get you the position with Helen. And who do you think covered your father's medical expenses last year?"

Emma's gaze shot back to Pamela. "He had insurance."

She shook her head. "The policy only paid a fraction of the cost. Wesley made up the difference."

"My father never said anything—"

"Because he doesn't know. Wesley never told him. I'm only telling you because I think you owe Wesley your loyalty."

"If what you say is true, then I'm very grateful for Mr. Corbett's generosity," Emma said. "And I'll pay him back every last cent. But I think your husband would be the first to agree that my loyalty should lie with his mother. She's my employer. If I feel there is something she needs to know, I'll go to her myself. Beyond that, as I said before, none of this is my business."

Emma hurried away before Pamela could detain her again, and as she let herself in through the French doors, she glanced back. The garden lights illuminated Pamela's face. Emma could see quite clearly the hatred that twisted the woman's lovely features, and an icy tingle lifted the hair at the back of her neck.

She had a terrible feeling that she'd just made a very sly and dangerous enemy.

the back of her seat.

She was almost feeling that she was just coming home, and that if the crowd...

Chapter Six

The meeting with the family wasn't as difficult as he'd anticipated. All those weeks David Tobias spent coaching him had prepared him well for the first round of grilling. He and Tobias had agreed that for as much as possible he would stick to the truth. That way he would be less likely to get caught up in a lie.

So that evening he found himself recounting to the family much of what had really happened to him during the past twelve years. He told them about his fledging construction business in New Orleans and how he'd been wiped out when the hurricane hit. The only thing he steered clear of was Tom Black's stint in a state prison.

"So you fell on hard times," Maris said with a compassionate smile. "There's no shame in that. Why didn't you contact us sooner? We're your family, Ash. We would have helped you out."

"Because I wasn't looking for a handout," he said. "I'm still not. You may find this hard to believe, but I'm not here because of the money. When I left here twelve years ago, I knew that I was burning my bridges. I didn't plan on coming back. At least not until I could prove to myself that I was my own man." He glanced at Helen. Her expression never changed, but he detected what might have been a telltale glimmer in her blue eyes.

"Then why did you come back?" Unlike the others, Wesley had refused to sit. He'd strategically placed himself by the fireplace so that he had the advantage of being able to survey the whole room at a glance. He was a perceptive man and he'd been watching his nephew like a hawk ever since he'd come into the room.

"I'm here because I heard about Grandmother's health. And because going through what I did in New Orleans made me face my own mortality. Life's too short to live with anger and regret."

"That's a very nice speech," Wesley said. "But what makes you think we'll just accept your word for why you're here?"

"I was wondering the same thing," Brad muttered. He got up and walked over to the bar to pour himself a fresh drink. When he didn't return to the sofa where he'd been sitting with his wife, Lynette got up and joined him.

Wesley's features hardened. "We've all believed for a long time that Ash was dead. And now here you turn up out of the blue claiming to be my long-lost nephew, yet you don't look very much like him. You say plastic surgery following a car accident changed your appearance. Okay. That sounds plausible. But you don't sound like Ash, either. You don't act like him. How do we know you're not an opportunist looking to cash in on my nephew's misfortune?"

"Enough!" Helen's cane thumped loudly against the hardwood floor. She hadn't spoken since she entered the room, but her blue gaze had never left Ash. Even when he was focused on someone else, he could feel those eyes piercing through his facade. "I'd like some time alone with my grandson."

"Mother, I really don't think that's a good idea," Brad said.

"Hell, no, it's not a good idea." Wesley came over and knelt beside Helen's chair. "We have to be careful. I know you want to believe he's Ash. We all do. But a lot's at stake here and not the least of which is your health."

"You let me worry about my own health," Helen said. "You've all had your turn. Now it's mine. I'm not taking anybody's word for anything. I'll have David Tobias arrange for a DNA test tomorrow, but right now, I would like a few words alone with this young man. Whoever he is."

Once everyone was gone and the doors to the library drawn shut, a measured silence fell over the room. He glanced at the old woman. In spite of her age and health, her posture was rigid and her eyes were focused like a laser beam on him.

Planting both hands on the cane, she leaned forward slightly. "Don't just stand there. Come over here and sit beside me so that I can get a good look at you."

He did as she said, and when he was settled at her side, her gaze raked over him again. "Wesley was right. You don't look much like my grandson," she said with a frown. "Oh, there's a strong physical resemblance, I'll grant you that. But there's something in your eyes…" She trailed off, her expression going hard. "You may be able to fool the others, but you can't fool me, young man."

He swallowed. "What do you mean?"

Her fingers tightened on the head of the cane. "You didn't come back because you fell on hard times. That's the one truthful thing you said all night. But I know the real reason you're here."

"You do?"

"You came back because you found out what it means to be a Corbett."

Her features softened almost imperceptibly, and then after a moment, he saw tears well in her eyes.

That surprised him.

And suddenly he knew exactly what to do. He picked up her hand and lifted it to his cheek.

AFTER HER CONFRONTATION WITH Pamela in the garden, Emma had gone straight up to her room to get ready for bed. But instead of putting on her nightgown after showering, she dressed in jeans and a light cotton shirt and headed back out again.

Tiptoeing down the hallway, she stole silently down the back stairway hoping to avoid anyone else who might still be up.

From her bedroom window, she'd seen the

flash of headlights as the family all left earlier. First Brad and Lynette, then Wesley and Pamela, and lastly Maris, who had probably stayed to see Helen off to bed. She might even have given her mother a mild sleeping pill to counteract the evening's excitement, which hopefully meant that Helen would sleep in the next morning and give Emma time to catch up on some paperwork.

Everyone was gone except for Ash. His car was still in the driveway and Emma assumed that he'd been invited to stay the night, if not move in permanently. As she slipped through the French doors in the parlor, her heart quickened...but whether in excitement or apprehension, she wasn't quite sure.

Pamela had been right earlier. If anyone could determine the man's true identity, it was Emma. She knew things about him that no one else did.

In spite of all the precautions she and Ash had taken that summer, Pamela had seen them together in the gazebo and Helen had guessed at her true feelings. But no one really knew what had gone on between Emma and Ash. No one could know the depth of their emotions or the secrets they'd shared... unless Ash had told them himself. And he would never have done that. Not the Ash Emma had known.

But that Ash was gone, she reminded herself yet again. The man she'd loved so desperately that summer was never coming back.

The moon was up, but once she left the garden, the grounds lay in deep shadow. Something rustled in the oleander bushes and she whirled in fear.

It was nothing. Just one of Helen's three-toed cats roaming the gardens. She kept half a dozen or so on the property, and Emma could see the amber gleam of the feline's eyes as he stalked his prey.

She watched for a moment, then continued down the path. Maybe she shouldn't be out so late, she thought nervously. She might be pressing her luck. Striving to overcome one's unreasonable fears was one thing, but it was quite another to deliberately tempt fate.

But the Corbett estate was ensconced behind stone walls and fences. She was safe here. She would never have come back if she thought otherwise.

The summerhouse was tucked away in a man-made grotto, landscaped with ferns and bromeliads and shielded from the upstairs window of the main house by banana trees and palms. A stream cut through the grounds and Emma could hear the sound of water trickling over well-placed rocks.

In this cool, lush fairyland, it was hard to imagine that the beach was so nearby, but the salty breeze that blew in from the gulf was a constant reminder.

One of Helen's cats had bedded down for the night in the airy pavilion, and when he saw Emma, his ears went back in alarm and he shot past her so quickly that she had to jump out of the way.

Then she stepped inside the rounded structure and stood in the center for a moment as memories closed in on her.

She hadn't been to the summerhouse since she'd come to work for Helen. Emma tried to fool herself into believing that she'd been too busy, but she had plenty of time for her walks and for reading in the garden. She could have made the short trek to the grotto if she'd really wanted to, but the truth of the matter was…she was afraid of this place. Afraid of the ghosts and memories. Afraid that she would never again find the kind of happiness she'd known here in Ash's arms.

And now he was back and the pull to the summerhouse had been irresistible tonight.

Emma stood for the longest time gazing through the arched openings into the darkness, her arms hugging her chest as she let the memories wash over her.

"I don't want to leave you tonight," Ash said to her. "I wish we could stay like this until morning."

Emma had propped herself on her elbow and smiled down at him. "We can't, though. My father would come looking for me, and if your grandmother ever found out about us—"

"I don't care if she finds out. She can't make me stop seeing you."

"She could cut you out of her will. You'd lose everything."

"No, I wouldn't. I'd still have you."

He curled his fingers around her neck and pulled her to him. Emma lay her head on his shoulder, splaying her hand over his bare chest so that she could feel the steady beat of his heart. It quickened as her fingers trailed down his stomach.

He caught her hand and drew it to his lips. "I love you, Emma."

"I love you, too," she'd said. "More than you'll ever know."

The sound of a snapping twig startled her out of her daydream, and Emma's heart pounded in alarm.

And then she saw him. He moved out of the shadows and for a moment he stood silhouetted in the doorway of the gazebo.

Slowly, he stepped inside. She couldn't see his face clearly, but she knew that he was staring at her. She felt the heat of his gaze pierce the walls she'd built around her heart and it frightened her. Excited her. She hardly dared breathe for fear he might disappear again.

He moved toward her and she closed her eyes.

"You remembered," she whispered.

THE BREATHY QUALITY OF HER VOICE was like a sensuous caress. He tried not to react to it because he didn't want to give her the wrong idea.

So instead he glanced around with a careless shrug. "Sure I remember this place."

His matter-of-fact tone caused her to falter. It was very dark inside the structure, but he had no trouble imagining the doubt flickering in her gray eyes. "Why are you here?"

"In the gazebo? I might ask you the same thing." He took another step toward her and she folded her arms as if putting a barrier between them.

I couldn't sleep," she said. "I felt like taking a walk."

"Another walk, huh?" He wished he could see her more clearly. He had to be very careful not to say or do the wrong thing, but it was hard to read her in the dark.

Maybe he'd made a mistake following her down here, but when he'd seen her slipping through the garden, he'd acted on impulse.

"I felt like taking a walk, too," he said.

She turned to him, her eyes glittering. "But why *here?*"

"Why not here?"

"You know why…."

Her voice trailed off on a note of suspicion, and he chided himself for forcing another meeting so soon. But if his own suspicions were right, the longer he waited the more dangerous she could become.

"I came because I thought you might be here and I wanted to talk to you. We barely had a chance to speak on the road earlier. I think we need to clear the air about a few things."

He sensed rather than saw her scowl. "Clear the air…about what?"

"About what happened twelve years ago."

He hated what he was about to do her, but it couldn't be helped. He had to remove her as a threat once and for all. It would be better for her in the long run, too.

Or had he read her wrong earlier on the road? Maybe she didn't still carry a torch for Ash Corbett, but he had to find out for sure. "I hurt you when I left and I'm sorry for that."

"It was a long time ago. It hardly matters now." But in spite of her denial, her voice trembled with emotion.

So his instincts were right. She'd been in love with Ash Corbett twelve years ago and she was still vulnerable to him today. She could still be hurt by him and that was the last thing he wanted.

"So you're over me," he said.

She gave a soft laugh. "Your ego astounds me. Of course I'm over you. We were kids, for God's sake."

"Then why have you never married?"

He heard her breath catch again. And then her voice hardened. "Why haven't you?" she shot back. "Or…did you?"

"No, I'm not married. But we were talking about you."

She shrugged. "I suppose I haven't met the

right man, but I'm hardly over the hill, you know."

He smiled. "So I noticed."

He felt a pang of regret as she reacted to his words. Moonlight flashed in her eyes as she looked up at him. "I can't believe you're really here."

"I know. I'm finding it a little hard to believe myself."

"Why did you really come back, Ash? Why now, after all these years?"

He hesitated, choosing his words carefully. "Probably for the same reason you did. I have roots here. And maybe I found out the hard way that when the chips are down, family is all that matters. Isn't that why you accepted my uncle's job offer? To be near your father?"

"How did you know that Wesley got me the job?"

"David Tobias told me. He filled me in on a lot of things that happened since I left. I'm sorry about your father. He's okay now, though, right?"

"Yes. He's doing a lot better, thank you."

"You two were always close. You must have been pretty scared when he got sick."

"I was. I don't know what I'd do if I lost him. He's all I have," she said softly.

"So you understand what I'm saying."

"Oh, I understand about family," she said. "But you were never that close to yours."

"I was a kid. I took a lot of things for granted. I'm not the same person I was back then."

"I can see that."

They both fell silent, and as his gaze drifted over her silhouette, he wondered what it had been like for her, loving a man who had apparently walked away without a backward glance. Had that betrayal made her reluctant to put her heart on the line again? Was that why she was still single?

He could tell she was guarded in the way she held herself, and for a moment, he was tempted to see if he could tear down those defenses.

Desire tugged at his resolve as he watched her in the dark, but he wouldn't give into it. No matter how attractive he found her, he couldn't afford to get close to her, and he couldn't allow her to wear her emotions on her sleeve. It was too dangerous...for both of them.

This had to end tonight but he couldn't be too heavy-handed. That might tip her off.

He could feel her gaze on him and he realized that he'd been silent for too long. He started to say something but she beat him to it.

"So how was it? Seeing your family again, I mean. Was it what you expected?"

He gave the matter some thought. "Yes and no. I suppose a part of me wanted to be welcomed back with open arms regardless of how much time has passed."

"You didn't really expect that, though. Not after letting everyone believe you were dead for twelve years. You're lucky your grandmother even let you in the house. You know how stubborn she can be."

The bitterness in her voice was like a slap across the face. He raked his fingers through his hair as he moved to the doorway of the gazebo and stared out at the darkness. Then he turned back to Emma.

"When I left here I never had any intention of returning. I thought it was best to make a clean break…from everyone. But like I said, things changed. Feelings changed. What appeared to be an impossible situation with my grandmother twelve years ago now seems like what it was…a spoiled kid throwing a temper tantrum because he didn't want to grow up and face his responsibilities."

"That doesn't sound like the Ash I knew talking," she murmured. "That sounds like Helen."

His voice hardened. "If you'd ever been down to your last nickel with no prospects in sight you might not be so quick to judge me."

"I'm not judging you," she rushed to assure him. "But back then you never cared about the money—"

"Because it was always there," he said with his own bitterness. "I've tried it the other way now and believe me, being your own man isn't all it's cracked up to be."

Her disappointment was tangible.

"So you didn't come back because you missed your family," she said slowly. "You came back for the money."

"It's the same thing. I see that now. I was born a Corbett. Running away didn't change who I am. It finally made me willing to accept it. Maybe even embrace it."

"Along with all that entails? The responsibilities? The expectations?" She shook her head, as if she still couldn't believe what he was saying. "You once told me that you would never accept the life your grandmother chose for you."

"And I didn't. I tried things my way. The choice to come back was mine and mine alone."

"I see." He heard the defeat in her voice,

and it gave him no pleasure to burst her illusions. He didn't want to hurt her, but letting her live in a fantasy world would be a far greater unkindness. The man she'd loved was probably gone forever. Maybe he could help her finally move on.

"Everyone said you'd changed, but I didn't quite believe it until now. When I saw you earlier…" She trailed off and looked away. "Twelve years is a long time, I guess. Longer than I realized."

He nodded. "You've changed, too, you know."

She touched her short hair. "So I've been told."

"I'm not just talking about your hair. You've lost the light in your eyes. Where did that go, Emma?"

"It doesn't matter."

"Of course, it matters. Just because we've both changed doesn't mean I don't care about you. I hope we can still be friends."

"Friends," she repeated numbly.

He resisted the urge to touch her chin, to lift her face to his. "We were best friends once, remember? And I have a feeling I'm going to need all the allies I can get in my corner."

It was a very long time before she spoke.

"You let me believe you were dead for all those years and now you come waltzing back into my life and expect me to be your *friend?*" Her voice broke with anger. "You've got some nerve."

She tried to move past him, but he caught her arm. "Let's get one thing straight." He paused before shoving the final dagger into her heart. "I didn't come waltzing back into your life. This is *my* life. My home. My family. I belong here whether you like it or not."

EMMA DIDN'T LOOK BACK AS SHE hurried away from the gazebo. From Ash.

She had no idea if he was somewhere behind her on the path or if he'd at least had the decency to allow her a moment to compose herself.

But it would take more than a moment for her to come to terms with what had just happened. In a single conversation, Ash had destroyed her dreams and diminished what they once had. And even worse, he'd made her ashamed for still caring about him.

How could she have been so stupid as to harbor, even for a second, the hope that he would still feel the same about her?

He'd been gone for so long and a lot had

happened to Emma in his absence. It was true that she wasn't the same person, either, but a part of her heart had been trapped in that summerhouse all these years.

A part of her had been waiting for Ash to come back so that they could pick back up where they left off. In her dreams, he'd never stopped loving her. He'd had a good reason for leaving, for disappearing without a word, but none of that would matter when they saw each other again.

Now, in the wake of their conversation, Emma saw things clearly for the first time in years. She'd clung tightly to that childhood fantasy because it was a defense, another wall she'd erected around her heart.

The torch she'd carried for Ash had given her an excuse to shy away from other men, to cut herself off from the possibility of an adult relationship.

She was scared to take a risk and so she'd convinced herself that Ash was the love of her life when in reality theirs had been nothing more than a summer fling, one that he'd probably forgotten the moment he left town.

And now he wanted to be her friend. A classic way of letting her down easy.

Emma's first impulse was to go straight to

her room, pack her bags, and get as far away from Jacob's Pass as she possibly could. She was hurt and humiliated and she dreaded the prospect of seeing Ash again, especially on a regular basis.

But running away never solved anything. Ash was proof of that, she supposed.

Maybe seeing him every day was the perfect way to get over him.

Because the man she'd confronted in the summerhouse was someone Emma didn't even much like.

THE DEED WAS DONE.

He sat smoking in the dark as he thought back over their conversation. Had he said anything to give himself away?

He'd been careful and pretty darn clever, if he did say so himself. All he'd had to do was let her take the lead and she'd revealed herself so easily.

A little too easily, he thought with a frown.

It was obvious that she'd never gotten over her first love, and he hadn't liked hurting her feelings. But he'd done it because it was necessary. He'd had no choice. He couldn't let her harbor the notion that there could still be something between them because if she got

too close—God forbid if he ever kissed her—
she would know the truth about him.

His cell phone rang, and he fished it out of
his pocket to check the caller ID. When he
saw that it was David Tobias, he wasn't going
to answer, but then changed his mind and
lifted the phone to his ear.

"Where the hell are you?" the lawyer thun-
dered.

"You don't sound happy."

"I'm not in the mood for games," Tobias
warned. "Just tell me where you are."

"I'm at the house."

"You're lying. I'm at the cabin right now.
Your car and clothes are gone. We had an
agreement, you son of a bitch. If I have to
track you down—"

"Relax." He flicked the cigarette through
the gazebo doorway. "I didn't run out on you.
I'm at the estate."

"The Corbett estate?"

"That's the only one I know," he said.

A long pause. Then Tobias said in a deadly
calm voice, "What have you done?"

The menace in the lawyer's tone was un-
mistakable and he knew better than to take it
lightly. David Tobias would be a very danger-

ous man to have as an enemy, and he had to be very careful about what he said and did.

"I've only done what you told me to do. You wanted Helen Corbett to accept me as her grandson. She's done that."

"You've seen Helen?"

"I left her a few minutes ago. We had a very poignant reunion, and now she believes I'm her grandson."

"Helen Corbett is nobody's fool," the attorney said suspiciously. "What did you say to her?"

"I let her do most of the talking. Then I gave her the story that we rehearsed and it worked like a charm."

"I don't believe you. You're up to something." Another tense pause. "Let me make something very clear to you. I'm a very powerful man in these parts. If you've double-crossed me, I will bury you. The raw deal you received in Louisiana will seem like nothing compared to the kind of justice you'll find down here. Do you understand what I'm saying?"

"Perfectly. But you don't need to worry about me. I did exactly what you told me to do."

"I told you to stay the hell put until the time was right," Tobias growled.

"Would Ash Corbett wait for you to give him the green light before seeing his grandmother?"

Tobias said nothing.

"That's what I thought. You and I both know he would have done exactly what I did."

"That may be, but I still don't like it. Any deviation from the original plan is an unnecessary risk."

"And you know as well as I do that for this plan to work, a certain amount of improvisation is necessary. You told me once that I had to live, breathe, sleep Ashton Corbett. That's what I'm trying to do. And evidently it's working because, like I said, Helen Corbett believes I'm her grandson."

"How do you know she's not just putting on an act to try and trip you up?"

"She's not."

"How can you be so sure? What exactly did you say to her to get her to accept you so quickly?" The suspicion was back in the attorney's voice. He was not going to let this go.

"Look, if you want me to be Ash Corbett, you've got to stop reminding me that I'm not. You've got to let me do this my way or Helen Corbett's going to see through both of us."

"That can't happen."

"Then give me some room to maneuver.

Ease up with the threats and don't expect me to remember every conversation word for word. If something comes up that you need to know about, I'll get in touch with you."

"My, my," the lawyer murmured sardonically. "If I didn't know better, I'd say you *were* Ash Corbett. And we both know what happened to him when he crossed the wrong person, don't we?"

A chill slid over him. "What do you mean? I thought you said he left home of his own accord."

When the lawyer didn't respond, the chill inside him deepened. But it was too late for second thoughts. He'd gone into this thing with his eyes wide open. He'd had his own reasons for accepting Tobias's terms, but with the darkness suddenly closing in on him, he was once again plagued by doubts.

"So what comes next?" he finally asked.

"Now we wait and see how the others accept your homecoming."

"We won't have long to wait. They were all here tonight. You'll probably be hearing from one or both of the uncles in the morning. If not sooner."

"Wesley and Brad were at the house tonight?" Tobias asked in alarm.

"Helen called the family together after your meeting with her this afternoon. She planned to announce the news of my homecoming after dinner, but my unexpected arrival threw a monkey wrench in her plans. I took everyone by surprise."

Tobias swore. "I still don't like this."

"So you said. But everything went down just the way you said it would. Maris was happy enough to see me. She's in my corner, but the uncles are going to be trouble."

"Because they have more to lose," Tobias said. Suddenly, he was all business again, as if his previous threats and cryptic remarks about Ash had never been uttered. "Especially Wesley. He's going to feel threatened by your homecoming so you'll have to be careful how you deal with him."

"Yeah, I got that impression. But somehow it's Brad that concerns me the most."

The lawyer scoffed. "Forget about Brad. Wesley is the one who holds all the power."

"That may be, but I sensed some pretty strong hostility in old Brad, and I don't think those hard feelings are all about the company or the power. If you ask me, he has a personal ax to grind with his nephew. You wouldn't be holding out on me, would you?"

"What do you mean?"

"Is there something about Ash's relationship with his uncle that you aren't telling me?"

"So far as I know the two of them had very little interaction. Both Wes and Brad had already moved out of the mansion when Ash came there to live. And then a couple of years later, Helen shipped the kid off to boarding school so he was barely even around except in the summers. If Brad had a problem with Ash it was probably a jealousy thing. Reese was always Helen's favorite, and then after he died, she turned to Wesley. When Ash came to live with her, she transferred her affections to him because he looked so much like Reese. Wesley didn't care so long as Helen gave him free reign at the company, but Brad has always been pushed aside. It's not surprising he'd be resentful."

"You sound sympathetic," he said. "Could it be that Brad is the one signing your check?"

Tobias gave a low laugh. "Nice try, but I told you before the identity of my employer—and yours—is not your concern."

"I like to know who I'm doing business with. You know the old saying. Lie down with dogs…"

"It's a little too late to worry about that," Tobias said.

"You just do as you're told and everyone walks away with what we want," the lawyer told him.

Everyone…except Emma Novick.

"Listen, there's something I need to tell you—" A rustle in the bushes startled him and he broke off.

"What's the matter?" Tobias demanded.

"I thought I heard something."

"Where are you?"

He didn't answer. Instead he sat very still peering into the shadows. Someone was out there. He could feel invisible eyes on him and the adrenaline that had been coursing through his veins all night spiked.

Had someone been listening to his conversation with Tobias?

Something shot out of the bushes toward him, so quick he jumped in alarm, and then he laughed.

"What's going on?" Tobias said anxiously.

"Nothing. I thought someone had overheard us at first, but it was just a cat."

"Are you sure?"

"Yeah. The damn thing is sitting in the doorway of the gazebo staring at me."

Tobias was silent for a moment, then he laughed, too. "You sound spooked."

"Let's just say, I'm not exactly a cat person. I'm allergic to them."

"Well, watch yourself, especially around Helen. You may have to take an antihistamine or something. You start sneezing she might get suspicious."

They talked for a few more minutes and then hung up. The cat was still watching him from the doorway and he said tentatively, "Here, kitty, kitty."

The cat got up and walked over to where he sat. Pausing briefly to sniff his ankles, the feline jumped up on the bench beside him, and then a moment later, resettled himself in Ash's lap.

Chapter Seven

Emma got up early the next morning and hurried downstairs, hoping that she could put in an hour or so at her desk before Helen made an appearance. She wasn't looking forward to facing her employer. Helen's warning the evening before still rankled, and if Emma had only herself to consider, she might have tendered her resignation on the spot.

But she had to worry about her father, too. After the scare with his heart attack, she wanted to be near him so that she could keep an eye on his health. The job with Helen was ideal because Emma could look in on him almost daily without compromising his privacy. And she knew that she would be hard-pressed to find a local position that paid as well, even if she relocated to Corpus Christi.

Besides, she'd already decided that running

away wasn't a viable option. For one thing, that was probably what Helen expected her do.

The woman could be extremely intimidating, even a little frightening, but her not-so-subtle coercion made Emma want to dig in her heels. It galled her that Helen apparently had no qualms about using her father's job as leverage after all the years of loyal service he'd given to the Corbett family.

Helen didn't want her grandson in a relationship with the hired help. Fine. Emma could deal with the woman's snobbery, but threatening her father's employment was beyond the pale.

And now Helen had created an awkward situation that was totally unnecessary because Ash had made it very clear last night that whatever had happened between him and Emma was in the past.

Emma had gotten the message loud and clear. She and Ash were over and it was time for her to move on. Helen had nothing to worry about in that regard.

But when Emma walked into the study that morning, she was met with Helen's cold, accusatory stare.

She decided not to let it throw her. Shaking off her lingering resentment and anger,

Emma mustered up a thin smile. "Good morning, Mrs. Corbett. You're up early I see."

"Which is more than I can say for some people," Helen snapped.

Emma made a point of glancing at her watch. She wasn't due at her desk for another hour or so and Helen knew that as well as she did.

Emma continued smiling through her irritation. "Well, I guess we're both early birds today."

Helen had been reading some contracts, but now she slid the legal documents aside and took off her bifocals. "You know that Ash is here."

It was a statement, not a question.

Emma nodded. "Yes. I saw his car in the driveway earlier."

Helen's mouth tightened almost imperceptibly at the corners. Carefully she sheathed her fountain pen. "Have you seen him?"

Emma was tempted to fib and say that she hadn't, but it was possible Ash had already said something to his grandmother.

"Only for a few moments. I was on my way back from seeing Dad last night when he drove up." That was true enough, although she supposed some might consider it lying by omission not to mention the summerhouse meeting. Emma considered it self-preservation.

Rising from her desk, she said, "Would you like for me to get you some coffee?"

Helen's lips thinned in disapproval. "No, thank you. I had my morning coffee with breakfast."

"You don't mind if I have some, do you?"

Without waiting for her to answer, Emma crossed the room to the silver coffee service that had been placed on a table near the window. She poured herself a cup, grateful to note that her hands were quite steady this morning. Surprising, considering everything that had happened in the last twelve hours.

She'd been threatened by her employer, her dreams had come crashing down around her and a woman she despised had tried to blackmail her into seducing her long-lost love.

Yes, that was quite a streak she was on.

She carried the coffee back over to her desk and turned on her computer as she sat down.

"Well?" Helen demanded.

Emma lifted an inquiring brow. "I'm sorry?"

"You said you saw Ash last night. I want to know what he had to say to you."

None of your business. "As I said, we only

spoke briefly. He seemed anxious to see his family and I didn't want to keep him."

Helen smiled at that. "He's a far different young man from the one who left here twelve years ago. You must have noticed it, too."

"Yes, I did."

Helen's gaze sharpened as she glanced at Emma. "It seems he finally has his priorities straight."

Her meaning couldn't have been plainer. Anger shot through Emma's bloodstream and she felt her cheeks color. Opening a file on her computer, she deliberately counted to ten before she responded. "Shall we get back to the letter we were composing yesterday when Mr. Tobias arrived? You wanted it to go out before the next board of directors meeting."

"The letter can wait."

"But the meeting is next week. If the letter doesn't go out today, the directors won't have much time to consider your points."

"That's not my concern at the moment."

Emma glanced up to find Helen's gaze still on her. "Is something wrong?" she asked hesitantly.

"You seem different this morning, Emma."

"I don't know why."

Helen continued to regard her from across

the room. Her expression seemed benign, but there was something in her eyes…in the set of her mouth…

Emma knew that look and she didn't trust it at all.

Helen was leading up to something, and it was a good bet that whatever was on her mind had to do with Ash.

Helen reached for her cane. Emma watched her struggle to her feet and make her slow, painful way over to the windows to glance out.

It was a long time before she spoke, and when she did, her voice was hard, cold. Resolved. "When Wesley told me that he'd made arrangements for you to come here and work for me, I wasn't enthusiastic about the prospect. To be truthful…" She turned to face Emma. "I told him that I would not have you in my home."

Her bluntness was a little hard to swallow, but Emma managed to hold on to her poise. "Why did you change your mind?"

"I didn't, but Wesley was adamant. To appease him, I agreed to give you a try, but I had every intention of letting you go when things didn't work out. I hadn't forgotten what had gone on between you and my grandson the summer before he left home."

"I had nothing to do with his leaving," Emma said, letting some of her anger creep into her tone.

"That may be, but I still had reservations about having you live here. My personal considerations aside, I also doubted that you would be able to handle the responsibilities. I remembered you as a young woman who always had her head in the clouds, and even though your work has been satisfactory these past few weeks, your manner has done nothing to disabuse me of that notion. I've never had much use for dreamers."

Emma folded her hands on top of the desk. "Are you firing me, Mrs. Corbett?"

The older woman lifted an eyebrow. "Firing you? No, I don't think that will be necessary. I can tell from your demeanor this morning that I got my point across last evening." She smiled slightly. "Or could it be that Ash got his point across?"

How did she know that? How the hell could she know about Emma's conversation with Ash last evening? No one had been in the summerhouse besides the two of them. The only person who could have told her was Ash himself.

Emma knew that it was crazy, but his betrayal was like a slap in the face. She had to struggle very hard not to show Helen how deeply her words affected her.

Helen walked back over to her desk and sat down. "Wesley needs these contracts before noon today," she said briskly, as if their previous conversation had never taken place. "I told him that I would have you drop them by his office this morning."

"Of course."

"You may as well count on taking the rest of the day off. Have lunch in town, shop, whatever you wish to do," Helen said magnanimously. "I won't need you for the rest of the day. I have plans with my grandson."

"Whatever you say, Mrs. Corbett." Emma stood. "I'll just go grab my purse."

She hurried out of the study, resisting the urge to glance over her shoulder to see if Helen watched her. Emma doubted it. Now that Helen had "gotten her point across," she wouldn't give Emma another thought.

ONCE IN HER ROOM, Emma hurriedly changed out of her business attire into a more casual skirt and sandals. If she was going to take the day off, she didn't want to be stuck in heels and a suit.

As she descended the curving staircase a

few minutes later, she saw Ash in the foyer gazing up at her. In spite of her earlier resolve, Emma's heart fluttered in awareness.

And in trepidation because under the cover of darkness, the changes hadn't been as noticeable. But now she understood why David Tobias had warned Helen to proceed with caution. The man who stood at the foot of the stairs was very different from the Ash she remembered.

Her Ash had been a devastatingly handsome eighteen-year-old, but now at thirty, he was older and harder looking.

However, his physical appearance wasn't the most stunning change. This Ash had a presence about him that was magnetic. Emma could feel the pull all the way down the stairs, and she clung tightly to the banister to make certain she didn't trip.

Was he Ash?

He had to be, didn't he? How would an imposter know about the gazebo?

She answered her own question. The same way Pamela Corbett had known.

He smiled as she neared the bottom of the stairs, and for one split second, Emma saw the old Ash in that smile. And then he was gone again.

"Good morning," he said.

"Good morning."

He nodded to her purse. "I see you're on your way out."

"I have an errand to run for your grandmother. I don't want to keep her waiting, so if you'll excuse me…"

"Emma." He touched her shoulder as she walked past him, then dropped his hand to his side.

Her heart skipped a bit as she paused and gazed up at him. "Yes?"

He wanted to say something to her. She could see it in his eyes, but he hesitated so long that Emma feared the moment was lost.

"What is it?" she prompted.

"About last night…"

She didn't want to talk about last night. She didn't need to experience that humiliation all over again. "I think we said all there is to say."

"Yes, that's the problem. Maybe I said too much. I didn't mean to imply that you don't belong here. This is your home as much as it is mine."

Her smile turned wry. "We both know that's not true."

"It is as far as I'm concerned. You and your father are an important part of this family.

You have every right to be here. Maybe even more than I do."

Emma shook her head. "My father and I work for your grandmother. We aren't part of your family, Ash. We're only here for as long Mrs. Corbett finds our work satisfactory. And since I don't want to lose my job, I'd better not keep her waiting."

"Emma—"

She didn't stop this time to find out what he wanted to say, but Emma had a feeling she'd be wondering about it for the rest of day.

She walked into the study without glancing back. Helen was still seated at her desk and gave no indication that she'd overheard Emma talking to Ash in the foyer.

"Here are the contracts," she said.

Emma accepted the packet and tucked it under her arm.

"I'll see you in the morning, Mrs. Corbett. Have a nice day."

"I plan to," she said without bothering to glance up.

When Emma turned to leave, she saw that Ash had followed her into the study. She hadn't heard his footsteps behind her, and now his presence startled her. She dropped the contracts and he bent to pick them up for her.

He gave her a lazy smile—the old Ash's smile—as he straightened and handed her the packet.

"Thank you," Emma muttered, thrown by that smile.

She hurried through the door and it wasn't until she was safely down the hall and away from those probing blue eyes—Ash's and Helen's—that she stopped for a moment to catch her breath.

Her pulse was racing, her heart hammering against her chest.

Dear God, she thought weakly. How had she ever doubted that he was Ash?

"I'M GLAD YOU'RE UP EARLY, ASH. We have a lot to do today."

He walked over to the coffee service, then turned hesitantly.

Helen nodded. "Help yourself."

"Thanks. I could use a hit of caffeine."

He carried his coffee to the window and glanced out. "It's a beautiful day," he said. "Maybe we could drive into town and have lunch near the water."

"We can have lunch here," Helen said flatly. "I'll have it served in the garden if you like."

He turned. "Are you sure? It might do you good to get out of this house for a while."

Helen scowled. "Since when are you so concerned about what is and isn't good for me?"

He shrugged again. "It was just a suggestion, Grandmother."

Her lips tightened as she regarded him across the room. "You wouldn't have an ulterior motive for asking me to lunch, would you?"

He grinned. "You mean like having you pick up the check?"

"I mean like a secret rendezvous with Emma."

He lifted his eyebrows in surprise. "What does Emma have to do with you and me having lunch in town?"

"Don't insult my intelligence, Ashton. You know exactly what I mean. I don't want you taking up with that girl again."

"Emma is hardly a girl. She's a grown woman in case you haven't noticed."

Helen's eyes glittered with anger. "Don't test me, Ash. I once told you that I would do whatever is necessary to keep the two of you apart. The same holds true today. Do you want to be responsible for putting her in the unemployment line? I'm sure she needs the money. And as for her father—"

"Stop it."

Helen's expression froze at his harsh command. Then her mouth tightened. "No one speaks to me in that tone—"

"No one blackmails me." He set aside his coffee and walked over to her desk. Planting his hands on the surface, he leaned toward her. "And no one tells me who I can and cannot see. Is that clear?"

She was livid. He could see the fury glittering in her eyes, but her facade never changed. "You will not see that woman while you are living under my roof."

"Fine." He straightened. "You and I both know other accommodations can be arranged quite easily."

They gazed at each other for a long, turbulent moment and then Helen glanced away. "I only want what's best for you, Ash. I always have."

"No, you want to run my life just the way you used to. But the rules have changed, Grandmother."

She gave him an imperious glower. "I don't like threats, either."

"I know you don't. But I'm not threatening you. I'm telling you to back off or I walk.

That's not a threat, it's a promise. My private life is off-limits."

"There are certain responsibilities that come with being a Corbett."

"I know about my responsibilities. If I weren't ready to live up to them, I never would have come back. But I won't have you meddling in my private life. You're just going to have to trust me when I tell you that I'll do the right thing. And as for Emma, you don't need to worry about her."

He walked back over and picked up his coffee cup. "I have no intention of starting a relationship with her."

Helen's blue gaze watched him closely. "I wish I could believe that, but I saw the way you looked at her just now."

"You saw what you expected to see," he said, calmly sipping his coffee. "Whatever I once felt for Emma Novick is long gone."

CORBETT ENTERPRISES OCCUPIED THE top six floors of one of the tallest buildings in downtown Corpus Christi. Most of the executive offices offered a panoramic vista of the gulf, and Wesley Corbett seemed absorbed in that view when Emma knocked lightly on his door.

He turned with a start. "Emma! I didn't know you were here. Come in."

"Victoria said you were expecting me," she said, referring to his secretary.

He nodded. "I just didn't know you'd make it so soon, but I'm glad you did. I want to get those contracts executed ASAP."

He moved away from the window and came to stand behind his desk. When Emma handed him the packet, he took out the contents, glanced through the contracts, then set them aside.

"Is there anything you'd like for me to take back to Mrs. Corbett?" Emma offered.

"No, not today. But don't hurry off. Have a seat. There's something I'd like to discuss with you."

Emma had a good idea what that something was. It was the same subject everyone seemed to want to discuss with her these days.

Hesitantly, she took a seat as she glanced around the plush office. The furniture was dark and traditional, the atmosphere almost somber. Except for the sweeping view and the brilliant light that came through the wall of windows, she would have found the space slightly oppressive.

But she had to admit the décor suited

Wesley. Even his wardrobe was classic and tailored, his ties understated and elegant. No touches of whimsy for him, although Emma knew firsthand that he had a sense of humor. He might be the only Corbett who did.

He sat down at his desk and regarded her thoughtfully for a moment. "You know my nephew's back."

Emma nodded. "I saw him briefly last night and again this morning. He was with Mrs. Corbett when I left the house."

"I was afraid of that. He's not wasting any time, is he?" Any touches of humor disappeared. His expression suddenly turned grim, as if he'd just been given very bad news. "I was dead set against mother letting him back into the house so soon. I think she should have waited until we have a chance to check him out."

"You sound as if you think he's an imposter," Emma said.

Wesley shook his head. "Oh, no. He's Ash all right. I yanked his chain a little about his appearance last night, but I knew who he was the moment I first laid eyes on him."

"Then…why are you concerned about him moving back into the house?" Emma asked.

"He may be my nephew, but I still don't

have any reason to trust him. He's been gone for over a decade. God only knows what he was up to during that time. He could be a criminal for all we know."

Emma stared at him in shock. "You're not implying you think he's dangerous, are you? Ash would never do anything to hurt Mrs. Corbett."

"He's already hurt her. What do you think he did to her twelve years ago when he left without a word? You don't think his little disappearing act and her years of subsequent worry helped bring on her stroke?"

Emma frowned. "That's not what I thought you meant."

Wesley picked up a gold pen and uncapped it. "Look, all I know is that he's been gone for a long damn time and now he shows up out of the blue claiming he wants nothing more than to be a part of this family again. I'm not buying it."

Emma wondered why he was telling her all this.

He recapped the pen, his forehead furrowing in thought. "It occurs to me that you're in a unique position, Emma."

So that was it.

"What do you mean?" she asked, even

though she knew exactly what he was getting at. He wanted the same thing Pamela wanted.

Emma was disappointed because she'd always given Wesley more credit than that. She knew that he was ambitious, but he'd always seemed like a decent man to her.

"I'd like for you to keep an eye on Mother."

"Mr. Corbett…" She paused, not wanting to offend him, but at the same time knowing she had to make it clear what she was and wasn't willing to do to keep her job. "I really appreciate everything you've done for me, but if you're asking me to spy on Mrs. Corbett, I don't think I can do that. You may have gotten me the job, but I still work for her. She needs to be able to trust me."

He looked slightly taken aback. "I wasn't suggesting that you spy on Mother. For one thing, she'd see right through it. And for another, I respect her too much to ever go behind her back like that. No, Emma, all I'm asking is that you keep an eye on her for me. If you think she's overdoing it or you see her strength waning, I want you to let me know about it. Or better still, call Maris. She's always been good at handling Mother. That's all I'm asking."

"I'm sorry," Emma said with an apologetic

shrug. "I didn't mean to jump to the wrong conclusion. It's just…" She trailed off.

He gave her a knowing look. "It's just that someone has already asked you to spy on her, is that it?"

Emma remained silent.

"You don't have to say anything. I have a pretty good idea of who it was." His mouth tightened. "You're absolutely right not to do this, Emma. Don't be intimidated or coerced. You work for Mother. No one else. If anyone approaches you about this matter again, you let me know. I'll deal with it."

"Thanks, but I think I made my position clear."

He nodded. "I'm sure you did. It goes without saying that I trust you. I would never have suggested you for the position if I didn't. But it's still gratifying to know that my faith wasn't misplaced. I appreciate your loyalty and I know Mother does, too." He tossed the gold pen aside. "Now enough about that. Mother tells me that she's given you the day off. You've probably made plans so I don't want to hold you up."

Emma started to rise, then sat back down. "Actually, there's something I'd like to talk to you about if you have a moment."

"Of course. What is it?"

Emma hesitated, not quite sure how to broach the subject. She decided to just be blunt. "I know that you paid for part of my father's hospital bills last year. I only found out recently, and I'm pretty certain my father doesn't know about it, either. Now that I do know, I want to pay you back."

Wesley shook his head. "That's not necessary."

"Yes, it is."

"Emma, it was nothing. Your father needed medical care and I was in a position to help him out. He's a good man. I wanted to make sure he got the best care he possibly could."

"And I don't mean to sound ungrateful." Emma's eyes filled with tears. "I'm thankful for everything that you've done for us, but I wouldn't feel right accepting charity."

"It's not charity. It was one friend helping out another. But I can see this has been weighing on you, so here's what we'll do. Once things calm down a little, I'll have the legal department draw up some sort of payment schedule for you. How does that sound?"

"I appreciate that." Emma stood. "I won't take up any more of your time."

"Emma?"

She turned back at the door. "Yes."

"I'll have the plan drawn up because it's what you want. But as far as I'm concerned we're even. I helped out your father and now you're helping my mother. I'm the one who's grateful."

Emma nodded, but a worrisome thought suddenly occurred to her. Was that the reason Wesley had gotten her the job at the mansion? Because he knew that once she found out about her father's medical bills, she would be indebted to him and therefore more cooperative when it came to reporting back to him about his mother?

Emma didn't want to believe Wesley could be so calculating. She'd always liked him, but when it came right down to it, he was still a Corbett. He was still his mother's son.

As she walked through the outer office, she waved goodbye to Wesley's secretary, then strode down the hall to the elevators. When she heard the ping, she stepped back to allow those inside room to get off. But when the doors slid open, there were only two people inside.

One was Pamela Corbett. The other was Brad.

His shirttail was askew and Pamela's hair

was all mussed. It took very little imagination to figure out what they'd been up to.

When they saw Emma, Brad quickly adjusted his clothing and stepped off the elevator, but Pamela merely smiled and took her time disembarking.

Emma entered the elevator and as she turned, she saw Brad glance over his shoulder. The menacing look on his face made her shiver, and she wondered if people underestimated him. If *she* had underestimated him.

He'd always seemed to fade into the background in Wesley's presence, but maybe his nondescript personality was a deliberate cover. Maybe Brad Corbett lived a double life. One of his personas was that of a younger brother who always deferred to his older, more dynamic sibling.

But the other…a cold, devious man who wasn't above conducting an illicit affair with his sister-in-law right under his brother's nose.

Chapter Eight

On her way back from Corpus, Emma called Laney Carroway and they agreed to meet in Jacob's Pass at a little seafood restaurant near the water. The place wasn't much to look at from the outside, but the picturesque view of the gulf made up for the lack of cachet. And Emma remembered the crab cakes being exceptionally good.

Laney was already seated by the time she arrived and she waved when Emma walked in the door.

"I'm so glad you called," she said when Emma had taken a seat across the table from her. "My shift doesn't start until four. You saved me from an afternoon with the soaps."

"And you saved me from having to prowl around in antique shops by myself," Emma said with a smile. She glanced around. "I haven't been here in years, but this place hasn't changed a bit."

"We came here on prom night," Laney said. "The boys wanted to get a bite to eat before we headed into Corpus."

"You're right. I'd forgotten all about that." Emma unfolded her napkin and spread it across her lap. "But I'm having a hard time remembering who our dates were that night."

Laney grinned. "Because we were both madly in love with other people at the time. I had a thing for Craig Thompson, but he'd asked Kristi Levitt to the prom. And you…" She gave a dreamy sigh. "You were still pining away for Ash Corbett."

Laney was the only person Emma had ever told of her feelings for Ash. They'd been best friends all through high school, but even Laney didn't know everything.

"That was a long time ago."

The waitress brought over two glasses of water and the menus, and Emma was glad for an excuse to change the subject. She opened her menu and glanced over the selections. "I wonder if the crab cakes are as good as I remember them."

"They are. I had them the last time I was

here. Myra never changes her recipes," Laney said, referring to the owner of the restaurant.

"Well, that's good to know." Emma continued to study the menu.

"Emma?"

She glanced up. "Yeah?"

A smile tugged at the corners of Laney's mouth. "You don't have to avoid the subject of Ash Corbett. I already know that he's back."

Emma's heart fluttered in spite of herself. "How do you know? Mrs. Corbett told me that she wanted to keep the news hush-hush for now."

"If I tell you, you have to promise not to repeat it to that old battle-ax. It'd be just like her to fire someone because they happened to let something slip in conversation."

"I won't tell her," Emma promised.

"In that case, it was Theresa Ramon's daughter. We work together at the hospital. We're both in pediatrics, and we've gotten pretty friendly over the years. She called me this morning when she heard about Ash from her mother. Theresa kind of let it slip by accident so Rachel swore me to secrecy. But give it another day or two and it won't matter anyway because it'll be all over town. If it isn't already," she said dryly. "You know how this place is."

Emma shrugged. "It's like any other small town."

"Yeah, people like to talk because there's not much else to do. But I have to admit, Ash Corbett returning from the dead is some pretty tasty gossip." She leaned forward and lowered her voice. "So have you seen him?"

Emma picked up her water glass. "Yes, I've seen him."

"Well?" Laney wiggled her fingers for more details. "What's he like? Is he still hot? What am I saying, of course, he's still hot. Those Corbett men only get better with age."

"Well, then, you just answered your own question," Emma said, again hoping to change the subject.

"Yeah, but I'm not letting you off that easy. Come on, Em. Give me the lowdown. The 411. And don't leave anything out. Where did you first see him and what did you say to him? And more important, what did he say to you?" Laney's eyes gleamed with expectation.

"Sorry to disappoint you, but there's really nothing to tell," Emma said. "I only saw him briefly last night and again this morning."

"And?"

"And what?"

"And *what?*" Laney looked at her in dismay. "You've been crazy about this guy since you were ten years old. He's all I heard about all through junior high and high school so you gotta give me something more to work with here. Are you still attracted to him?"

"He just got back, Laney. I've barely spent any time with him at all. And besides, after twelve years, we're pretty much strangers to each other."

"*Strangers?* But you must still feel *something* for him." Laney tucked a strand of blond hair behind one ear. "Rachel said that he was in some sort of accident and he had to have plastic surgery. Her mother told her that he doesn't look anything like he used to. Is that true?"

Emma thought about it for a moment. "He looks different but he's still Ash."

Laney sighed again. "That's what I figured. I didn't think he could have changed that much. He used to be our version of McDreamy, remember? Those blue eyes with that dark hair…" She gave Emma a sly smile. "I used to be so jealous of you, you know. I thought your hooking up with Ash Corbett made you just about the luckiest girl in the world."

Emma frowned. "You didn't need to be jealous of me. Nothing was ever going to come of that romance. Helen wouldn't let it." She winced at the bitterness in her voice. Why was she letting the past get to her so much? Why did it still matter that she'd never measured up to Helen's expectations for her grandson?

"I know, but that's what made it so romantic," Laney said. "You were like star-crossed lovers or something." She made a gagging sound. "Did I just say that? That was cheesy."

"Yes, it was. I think you need to step away from the soap operas," Emma said with a grin. "Join us back here in the real world."

"Okay, so I get a little carried away sometimes." Laney shrugged. "There are worse things." Her gaze shot to the front of the restaurant and she straightened in her seat. "And speaking of romance…"

Emma glanced over her shoulder to see who had attracted Laney's attention. The only person she saw was a man in a county sheriff's uniform. He'd just walked into the restaurant and was waiting to be seated.

She turned back to Laney. "Isn't that Rick Bledsoe?"

"Yes, and doesn't he look hot in that uniform? He's got the tightest little butt."

Emma started to turn back around, but Laney reached across the table and grabbed her arm. "Don't keep looking back! He'll know we're talking about him."

"Sorry."

"Just be cool." Laney opened her menu but she continued to surreptitiously watch Rick over the edge. "He got divorced last year and I've been dying for him to ask me out."

"Why don't you ask him out?" Emma suggested.

"I just might if I could ever get him alone. One of us is always on duty when we bump into each other. The timing just hasn't worked out."

"What about now?" Emma said. "Looks like he's having to wait for a table. Why don't you go ask him to join us?"

"You wouldn't mind?"

Emma glanced back down at the menu. "Sure, go ahead if you want to. I always liked Rick."

"Just don't get any ideas," Laney warned with a wink as she slid out of her chair. "I saw him first."

Emma smiled at the good-natured banter. It felt really good to be out socializing with

friends her age. She hadn't realized how sequestered she'd been at the mansion for the
past couple of months. The errands she ran
for Helen got her out and about, and she had
her evening walks and dinners with her father.
But she hadn't had lunch with a friend, much
less a date, in far too long.

Her solitary lifestyle had started in Dallas
after the attack. She'd stopped going out with
friends and instead had locked herself in her
apartment every night, afraid to venture out
any farther than her mailbox.

But Emma saw now how damaging that
behavior had been and how it fit a pattern for
her. For one reason or another, she'd been
putting her life on hold for as long as she
could remember.

It was time for that to stop.

"Emma, you remember Rick."

She roused herself from her reverie and
glanced up. "Of course. Hi, Rick. It's good
to see you again."

"Hey, Emma." He paused. "Are you sure
I'm not intruding on your lunch? You
probably have a lot of catching up to do."

"Oh, we've already done that," Laney
hurried to assure him. "Right, Emma?"

"Right." She smiled at Rick. "Sit down. We'd like you to join us."

He took a seat beside Laney and laid his hat in the empty chair next to Emma's. "So what are you two up today?"

"We were just talking about what we wanted to do after lunch, weren't we, Em? I don't have to be at work until four so I have the whole afternoon." Laney's smile was anything but subtle.

"And what about you, Emma?" Rick asked politely.

"I have the day off, but I'll probably head back home after lunch—" She broke off with a grunt when Laney kicked her under the table. She shot her friend a surprised look, and Laney gave her a half-hearted smile.

"Sorry, my foot slipped," she muttered. "There's not much room under these tables."

"No, they pack 'em in here pretty tight," Rick agreed.

He motioned for the waitress. "Have you ordered yet?"

"No, we were just about to."

The waitress was a young, pretty college-age girl who flirted openly with Rick as she took their orders. Emma could almost see the smoke rolling out of Laney's ears the longer the girl tarried.

Finally she had everything she needed and turned to hurry off toward the kitchen. And Laney wasted no time trying to recapture Rick's attention.

"What were we talking about? Oh, yeah, our plans for the rest of the day. As it happens, Emma and I are both free as birds all afternoon. What about you?"

"I'm still on duty," he said. "My watch doesn't end until five."

Laney's face fell. "That's too bad. I was hoping the three of us could go down to the beach for a while. Be just like our high school days. We could even take a cooler. I've been wanting to work on my tan."

Rick shoved his water glass aside and leaned an arm on the table as he regarded Laney. Emma didn't see how he could resist her. Her smile and bubbly personality were adorable. Even her blatant flirting was charming.

"I don't have time to go to the beach," he said. "But we could take a boat ride if you want."

Laney's eyes lit with excitement. "A boat ride? I love boats! What do you have in mind?"

Rick glanced at Emma, and the quick

shadow that flickered in his eyes made her dread what he was about to say.

"I'm going out to Shell Island this afternoon. You and Emma can ride along if you want."

Emma's breath quickened, and she opened her mouth to decline the invitation. But Laney was already accepting for both of them.

"That sounds like fun! I haven't been out to Shell Island in years," she said. "We'd love to go, wouldn't we, Em?"

"I don't know—"

"Oh, come on. It'll be fun."

Emma glanced at Rick. "Why are you going to Shell Island?"

"It's in our jurisdiction," he explained. "We make a run out there every so often to try and keep the vandals away."

"What's it like now?" she found herself asking.

He shrugged. "Pretty much the way it's been for years. The houses are still standing, although some of the roofs have caved in."

"What about the church?"

It was on the stone steps of that church that Emma had experienced the strongest premonition. It was inside that church that the first body had been discovered. She couldn't help shuddering at the memory.

"I know what you're thinking," Rick said. "I was a little uneasy the first time I had to go out there by myself. But there's nothing to be afraid of. It's just land with some old houses on it. Whatever happened there years ago…that's all in the past. I'm surprised some developer hasn't snapped it up and tried to build a subdivision out there or something. It's actually a real pretty little island."

Somehow Emma doubted that. Shell Island would always be a dark, foreboding place to her. A place that still haunted her dreams from time to time.

But Rick was right. Whatever darkness had inhabited the island in the past was long gone. People were evil. There was no reason to be afraid of a place.

Maybe a trip out there in broad daylight with an old friend and a deputy sheriff might be just the thing to exorcise a few more of her demons.

"Okay, I'll go," Emma said, but her stomach was so tied in knots that she could hardly eat her crab cakes.

THE RIDE OUT TO SHELL ISLAND took only a few minutes, but by the time Rick pulled the boat alongside the dilapidated peer, Emma had decided that she'd made a big mistake. She never should have come out here.

She tried to tell herself that she was over-reacting. There was nothing to be afraid of anymore. All the bodies were gone and nothing had been found out here in years. Like Rick said, Shell Island was just a piece of land with some old houses on it.

At one time the island had been home to a thriving community, but it wasn't the ghosts of those who had lived there that haunted Emma.

Twelve years ago, six bodies had been found on the island. In a course of five years, those six young women had been taken to the island never to be heard from again. Some-one had brutally murdered them and the killer had never been caught.

And eighteen years prior to that, Mary Ferris's mutilated body had washed up in the bay. For all anyone knew, she could have been murdered on the island as well.

That the killer hadn't struck again for over a dozen years did nothing to put Emma's mind at ease. Because he was still out there somewhere. And there could be more bodies buried somewhere else.

The sun beat down hot on her shoulders, but she couldn't stop shivering.

Rick tied up the boat, then offered his hand down to Laney.

She laughed with nervous excitement as she scrambled upon the pier. "Wow, this place really is kind of creepy, isn't it?"

"We haven't even left the pier yet," Rick teased her. "Way until you see the houses."

"I thought you said it wasn't scary anymore," Emma said. She hadn't yet climbed out of the boat. She wasn't sure she was going to. "Maybe I'll just wait for you two here."

Rick gave her an encouraging smile as he held out his hand. "I didn't mean to scare you like that. Come on. It's a pretty interesting place. There's nothing to be afraid of."

Famous last words. Emma grabbed his hand and let him help her up to the pier.

The island was tiny, but the vegetation had grown up so high that the houses weren't visible from the beach. Rick took the lead down a narrow path through the fan palms and oleanders.

As they walked along single file, Laney glanced back and mouthed a thank-you to Emma. Then she jerked her head in Rick's direction and put a hand over her heart. *I think I'm in love.*

Emma just shook her head, but Laney's

silly pantomime helped dispel some of the uneasiness that had been hovering over her ever since Rick had mentioned the island.

A few yards inland, they came to the first house. Like all the other homes on the island, it was a single-story clapboard building with rickety steps leading up to a covered porch. The front door sagged open and most of the windows had been broken out years ago.

The shards of glass that remained in the frames reminded Emma of jagged teeth in yawing mouths. And the windows above it were the eyes....

She rubbed her hands up and down her arms, trying to ward off a lingering chill. It was just an old house. It didn't have teeth or eyes and it couldn't watch her, although she had the strangest sensation of *being* watched. She glanced over her shoulder, her gaze scouring the thick brush.

Laney grabbed her arm and Emma jumped.

"Oh, you really are spooked, aren't you? Come on." She tugged on Emma's hand. "Let's go take a look inside."

"You two can have a look around here while I go check out the church," Rick said. "That's usually where the vandals concentrate their mischief. But if you go inside the house, watch your step. Some of the floor-boards are rotting through. And don't wander off too far. I'll be back in a few minutes. If you want, I can give you a quick tour of the island before we leave."

Laney went up the porch steps first and glancing over her shoulder, motioned for Emma to follow. "Don't you want to see what's inside?"

"Not really."

But Emma had to admit a part of her was curious. And now that she'd had a little time to adjust to being on the island, she realized that much of the creepy atmosphere she re-membered from her trip out here before really had been exaggerated in her mind.

There was nothing dark or menacing about the place. The sun was shining and the olean-ders bloomed in profusion. The vanilla-like fragrance hung on a warm, balmy breeze that blew in from the gulf.

All these years, she'd been afraid of this place for no reason, Emma realized. It really was a very pretty little island.

She followed Laney up the steps and the two of them walked inside. Even with the broken windows, the tiny rooms were dim and slightly claustrophobic. The floorboards squeaked ominously under their feet as they walked from room to room, and Emma tried to tread lightly. The house was set up off the ground. If she fell through a rotting floorboard, she could easily break a leg.

There was nothing much to see inside. Just a few tattered books and some old clothing that had been left behind. Emma picked up one of the mildewed books and glanced at the spine. It was an old history book.

"Hey, come take a look at this!" Laney called from another room.

Emma dropped the book and wandered back out into the corridor. "Where are you?"

"Down here. I think this must have been one of the bedrooms. You'll never believe what's in here."

She sounded too calm for her discovery to be anything dire, Emma decided. She followed the sound of Laney's voice to the end of the hallway. The door was open and Laney stood in the center of the room.

"Check it out," Laney said and spreading out her arms, slowly turned in a circle.

Emma couldn't imagine at first what she was doing, but then she looked down and saw that Laney stood in the middle of what looked to be a pentagram.

A red pentagram.

A spray can had been discarded nearby and Emma let out a breath of relief. For a moment she'd actually thought the symbol might have been drawn in blood. *Crazy.*

"How long do you suppose it's been here?" Laney said, making no move to step out of the symbol.

"The paint looks fairly fresh." Emma was surprised at how calm she sounded. "That area doesn't have as much dust as the rest of the floor."

"I wonder if Rick knows about this. I should probably go find him and tell him."

"And leave me here?" Emma blurted, giving away her nerves.

"You can come, too, if you like." But Laney's tone clearly conveyed her desire to be alone with Rick Bledsoe. "There's nothing to be afraid of. I'm sure it was just some kids fooling around."

She was probably right. After all, the culprit had left his spray paint can behind. That hardly seemed ominous. "Rick said he was going to the church. Do you even know where it is?"

"I've been out here a few times. I remember the general layout of the island,

and besides," Laney said, grinning, "I have a sixth sense about these things. I'll find him, don't worry. But if I'm not back in an hour, send out a search party."

"If you're not back in an hour, I'm taking the boat back to town," Emma warned.

She followed Laney back out to the porch. At the bottom of the steps, Laney paused and glanced up at her. "Are you sure you don't mind? I know you only came out here because I asked you to and now I'm abandoning you. But this is the first chance I've had to be alone with Rick in ages. And I really like him, Em."

Who was she to stand in the way of romance? Emma thought. Or lust, whatever the case might be. "Go on," she said with a careless shrug. "I'll be fine."

After all, she was a grown woman. If she couldn't stand to be by herself for a few minutes in the middle of the afternoon, she had bigger problems than she thought.

EMMA LASTED FIVE MINUTES ON the porch and then she decided that she really didn't care if she interrupted Laney's only opportunity to be alone with Rick or not. She didn't want to wait at the house by herself because she was starting to get a little spooked again.

Maybe it had been teenagers who'd painted the pentagram on the floor of the bedroom, but given the island's history, Emma wasn't going to beat herself up for being a little shaken by the symbol.

She considered just heading back to the boat to wait for the other two there, but as she lingered on the porch, her gaze swept over the scenery and she glimpsed the roof of the church peeking through the vegetation. That was where Laney and Rick were.

Emma didn't remember it being so close to the beach, but she'd only been thirteen when her father brought her out here to look around. She didn't remember the island being so overgrown, either, or the houses being in such poor shape. But they must have been because no one had actually lived on Shell Island since the fifties.

As Emma stood there staring at that roof, she tried to remember everything she'd read about the island back then. It had been inhabited by a handful of families who shunned modern conveniences. Most of the men had been fishermen, but a few had been day laborers in town. The women hadn't been allowed to work off the island, and the children had been home-schooled.

Even when they came into Jacob's Pass for supplies, the islanders didn't mingle with the townspeople. They took care of their business as speedily as possible and returned by boat to their homes.

Then one by one, for whatever reason, the families left the island and some of them settled around Corpus Christi. Others moved farther away, and so far as Emma knew, no one had kept track of their whereabouts.

But the rumors about the families had persisted for years. When Emma's class studied local history in junior high school, she'd been amazed by all the stories of dark ceremonies, animal sacrifices and ritualistic worship. For a while it had almost been a contest to see who could come up with the most bizarre tale.

Emma had absorbed it all, and when her father had brought her to the island to look around, her imagination had been primed.

For a long time, she tried to convince herself that those stories had accounted for the awful sense of foreboding that had gripped her as she and her father walked from house to house. Those stories were the reason she'd been too scared to enter the church.

But years later when a body had been found in that same church, Emma wondered

if what she experienced had been some sort
of premonition.

As she stood on the porch now, she waited
for that same sense of dread to return. But all
she felt was a vague uneasiness. And, yeah,
a little fear. She was anxious to leave the
island, but it was nothing like the terrible pre-
sentiment she'd experienced before.

Trotting down the porch steps, she headed
down the path toward the church. She'd just
take a quick look. Laney and Rick were
probably still there so she might not even go
inside. She just wanted to see what the place
looked like.

As Emma emerged into the clearing a few
minutes later, she paused, her gaze raking
over the structure. It was a long, one-story
building that extended back into the thick
vegetation, giving it the appearance of a man-
made tunnel. Unlike the houses, the church
set flush to the ground, but the stoop was
elevated and the area underneath was littered
with beer cans and debris.

The church was in better shape than the
houses because the walls were stone. But the
windows here had been broken out, too, and
the walls were covered with graffiti.

Taking a few steps toward the building,

Emma called out Laney's name and then Rick's. When neither answered, she climbed up the steps and pulled on the door. It swung back on squeaky hinges, and the sound sent a shiver up Emma's spine.

"Laney? Rick? Are you in here?"

She stood in the doorway and glanced inside. The interior wasn't anything like she imagined it would be. She'd always pictured a dark, cold room filled with creeping shadows.

In reality, sunbeams danced through the gaping windows, filling the whole place with light. The walls were white stucco, which added to the airy feel of the interior. It was a large room, spacious enough to accommodate all the families that had once lived on the island and then some.

The building really wasn't scary at all, Emma decided. Unless she thought about the body of the young woman that had been found inside. But that was twelve years ago. Nothing had happened on the island since then.

And Emma had to admit that she was curious about the church. She'd thought about it for so long. She'd even had nightmares about it. And now here she stood on the threshold.

She took a step inside and gazed around. Most of the furnishings had been destroyed or hauled off a long time ago, but a few battered rough-hewn pews remained, only because transporting them back to the mainland would be difficult. Some of them were overturned, and Emma could see where initials had been deeply carved into the bottoms. The dais from where the sermons had been delivered was gone, as was the altar.

There really was nothing much left to see. Just an empty room with a few cobwebs and some expletives scrawled on the walls.

Emma was suddenly glad that she'd come. She felt a weight lift from her shoulders.

All these years, she'd been carrying around a terrible guilt. If she'd told someone about the premonition she'd experienced on the island, perhaps those young women's lives could have been saved.

But now she realized how foolish she'd been to take that kind of responsibility on herself. Whatever had happened to those poor victims had nothing to do with her. She could have done nothing to save them.

And this place…really was just a place. If evil had been here, it was long gone now.

Emma rubbed her hands up and down her arms, not because she was frightened, but because it was cool inside the stone building.

She wondered where Laney and Rick had gone off. Had she missed them on the path? Maybe they were back at the first house waiting for her.

As Emma turned to leave, a strong breeze swept in through the broken windows, and the door swung shut with a *bang*.

Chapter Nine

Emma's pulse jumped to her throat as she whirled.

It was nothing, she told herself quickly. The draft had blown the door shut

And then as she reached for the door, she heard something behind her. The telltale rustle lifted the hair at the back of her neck. Someone was in the church with her.

"Rick? Laney?"

Emma's heart started to pound as she slowly turned to scan the room.

No one was there. The space was bright enough that she would have been able to see someone, even if they lurked in one of the corners.

Emma knew that she was letting her imagination get the better of her again, but she didn't care. Suddenly she couldn't wait to get out of the church.

Putting a hand on the door, she tried to push it open, but the heavy wood wouldn't budge. She tried again and again.

Panic mushroomed in her chest as she put her shoulder against the door and shoved with all her strength. It still wouldn't give.

Frantic now, she beat on the wood with her fists. "Laney! Rick! Are you out there? The door's stuck!"

She kept at it until her throat grew raw and her knuckles were sore. "Help!"

Finally she gave up and turned to lean heavily against the door as she surveyed the room. There had to be another way out. The windows were fairly high, but she could drag one of the old pews over and climb up. All she had to do was find something to break out the rest of the glass.

There was no reason to panic. She could get out of here.

But another thought suddenly occurred to her. What if Laney and Rick had already gone back to town? What if they'd left her here?

Calm down.

They would never do that. They'd only been separated for a few minutes. They wouldn't leave her. Not without searching the island for her first.

Emma headed for one of the windows, but the rustling sound grew louder. She halted in her tracks, her mouth going dry with fear.

She knew she was probably overreacting, but she couldn't help it. A woman's body had been found inside that church. Five other bodies had been buried nearby. The women hadn't just been murdered. They'd been tortured, their bodies badly mutilated.

They may have even been killed in this very room.

What was she thinking, coming out here like this? Emma thought nervously. There was a reason why she'd had nightmares about this place.

Her father was right. She didn't have to prove her courage. What happened to those women wasn't her fault and the assault in her apartment hadn't been her fault, either. She hadn't fought off her attacker because he'd held a knife to her throat.

"Chances are he would have killed you if you hadn't done as he said, Emma," her father had reasoned. "You did the right thing."

"Yes, but he might have killed me anyway if my neighbor hadn't called the police," she'd answered. "And I would have died without fighting back."

There was no use going over that again, Emma told herself firmly. She couldn't change the past.

Besides, all she cared about now was finding a way out of the church—

The door flew open behind her and Emma screamed.

"Hey, it's okay," Rick called. "It's just us."

Laney hurried past him and put her hand on Emma's arm. "Are you okay?"

Emma nodded and let out a shaky breath. "The door was stuck. I guess…my imagination kind of ran away with me."

"I'm not surprised." Laney glanced around and shivered. "This is where it happened, isn't it?"

"This was where they found one of the bodies," Rick said. "I don't think the victim was killed in here, though."

"Why do you say that?" Emma asked.

"I've had a look at the files. There wasn't enough blood or forensic evidence found at the scene. The women were probably slain someplace else and the killer dumped the bodies out here thinking they'd never be found."

"But he buried all the others. The last one was found in here," Laney said. "If I remember correctly, the medical examiner from Corpus said the victim hadn't been dead that long." She hugged her arms around her middle, evidently feeling the same creeping chill that Emma did.

Rick shrugged. "He probably would have buried her, too, but he may have run out of time. Maybe he figured on coming back out in a day or two and burying her with the others. But she was found before he could return."

"And just think," Laney said in a hushed voice. "Whoever did it is still running around loose. It could be someone we know. Even someone we work with. Someone we see every day." Her gaze shot to Rick and he threw his hands up.

"Hey, I hope you're not putting me on your suspect list. I was just a kid when those bodies were found."

"Emma and I were seventeen and since you were two years ahead of us in school, you must have been nineteen. Not so young really. The newspapers said the women were killed in a five-year span, give or take. So you would have been fourteen at the time of the first murder."

"I hope you don't seriously think I had something to do with those killings," Rick said. "Not after…"

They exchanged a glance and Laney laughed. "Of course not. I was just proving a point. The killer could be anyone. Even someone we least expect."

"Or he could be a stranger," Rick said. "It's unusual for a serial killer to hunt in his own backyard. Like I said, those women were probably killed elsewhere and brought here for disposal."

Emma had been silent for a long time, but now she said with a shiver, "Could we talk about this somewhere else. I've had enough of this place."

"Right." Rick stepped back so that she could exit in front of him. "You two can wait outside. I'll just have a quick look around and then we'll head back."

"Be careful," Emma said. "I heard something rustling around back there. It was probably just a mouse, but it could be a snake."

"I'll check it out."

As the two women walked down the steps, Laney took Emma's arm. "Are you okay? The way you screamed…I thought something awful had happened."

"I kind of panicked when I couldn't get the door open," Emma admitted. "But I'm okay now."

"I'm sorry I ran off and left you like that," Laney said contritely. Then she gave Emma a sly smile. "But for what it's worth, Rick Bledsoe is one great kisser."

WHEN THEY GOT BACK TO JACOB'S PASS, Laney glanced at her watch and gave a little shriek. "I have to get going or I'll be late." She gave Emma a quick hug and said in her ear, "Thanks for going with me. I owe you one."

"I'll remember that," Emma promised.

"What about your car?" Rick asked. "It's still at the restaurant, isn't it?"

"No, I walked over. And my apartment is just a couple of blocks from here. I can probably get there just as fast on foot. Ciao!"

She sprinted across the street and then waved again before disappearing around a corner.

Rick said awkwardly, "Look, I'm sorry about what happened back there on the island."

"Oh, don't think anything of it," Emma said with a shrug.

"If I'd known you were that jumpy, I never would have left you alone for so long. Laney and I got to talking…." He seemed a little uncomfortable about whatever had happened between them.

Emma smiled, trying to put him at ease.

"Don't worry about it. Like I said, my imagination got the better of me when I couldn't get the door open, but I'm fine now. No harm done."

"Are you sure? Because you still look a little shaky."

"Yes, I'm sure." She glanced at her watch. "It is getting pretty late. You probably need to get back to the station and I should head home."

"I know you left your car at the restaurant. At least let me give you a ride back."

Emma slung her purse over her shoulder. "You don't have to do that. I can walk. It's not that far."

"I go right past the restaurant on my way to the station. Come on. It's the least I can do for dragging you out to the island."

"You didn't drag me. I wanted to go."

But Emma didn't try to argue anymore. She climbed into his squad car and a few minutes later, he pulled into the restaurant parking lot.

Emma started to get out, then she turned back to Rick. "Can I ask you a question?"

"Sure. What is it?"

"You said you read the files of those murders twelve years ago. What about the teacher who was killed before that…Mary Ferris. Do you think she was murdered by the same person?"

"So far as I know there was never any evidence to tie her murder to the others. That was what? Thirty years ago? They didn't have the kind of forensic collection and DNA testing that we do nowadays. We'll probably never know if that kill was related to the others or not."

Emma hesitated. "What about the woman who was found in the bay a couple of months ago…Ann Webster? Laney and I saw you the day she was dragged out of the water, remember?"

"Her husband was charged with the murder."

Emma nodded. "I know. I heard he confessed."

"More or less." Rick's gaze broke from hers and he glanced out the window. "There's been some speculation recently that he might have been coerced into that confession."

"By whom?"

Rick's gaze came back to Emma's. He looked troubled and more than a little angry. "I can't say anything more about the case. I will tell you this. That son of a bitch is guilty and if he gets off on a technicality, someone's going to come after his murdering hide."

Emma was startled by his passion. "The evidence against him is that strong? There's no possibility that he could be innocent?"

Rick frowned. "What are you getting at, Emma?"

"I guess I'm wondering if it's possible that the person who killed those women twelve years ago could have killed Ann Webster?"

"No way. Derrick Webster is guilty as hell. Besides, twelve years would be a long time between kills."

"Mary Ferris was found eighteen years before those bodies were uncovered on Shell Island. I've heard of serial killers who go dormant for long periods of time," Emma said. "It is possible, right?"

He stared at her for a moment. "Why are you dwelling on all this ghoulish stuff? It's history."

Emma shrugged. "I know, but something that Laney said earlier has been bothering me. The killer is still out there. He could be someone we know, someone we work with, someone we see every day."

"I think you and Laney have been watching a little too much *CSI*," he said dryly. "Ann Webster was murdered by her no-good husband. As for the others…like I said, history. You should just forget about it, Emma. You think about stuff like that too much, it'll give you nightmares."

She tried to smile. "You're probably right. Anyway, thanks for the ride, Rick."

"Anytime."

She started to climb out of the car, then turned back. "You know, this is really none of my business, but Laney's a great person."

"No argument there." He stretched his arm across the back of the seat. "She comes on a little strong sometimes, though. I'm not used to that."

"Maybe you should be flattered," Emma said. "She's a beautiful woman."

"Yeah, she is." He stared out the windshield, his gaze narrowing in the glare. "As long as we're getting personal here…" He turned back to Emma. "I've wanted to call you ever since I heard you were back in town."

Oh, no, Emma thought. She hadn't expected this.

"Now I'm the one who's flattered," she murmured. "But, Rick, Laney is my friend. I really don't think we should have this conversation."

"I know. You two were big buddies all

through high school. But the truth of the matter is, I always had a thing for you, Emma. Just never had the nerve to tell you."

Emma was at a loss. "I had no idea."

"I guess it's just my bad luck that Laney chose now to take an interest in me."

"Most men wouldn't consider that back luck," Emma said.

"I realize that. But I always seem to come up a day late and a dollar short in the romance department." He gave her a weak smile. "You can't blame a guy for trying, right?"

EMMA COULDN'T BELIEVE IT. All she wanted to do was get home and relax for a while in her room, but her blasted car wouldn't start. When she turned the key in the ignition, the engine groaned but wouldn't kick over. She tried a few more times, then grabbed her cell phone from her bag to call her father.

Someone rapped on her window and she rolled the glass down, thinking it was Rick. But she was shocked to see Ash staring down at her. She hadn't even seen him drive up.

He propped his arm on the roof and leaned in. "Need some help?"

Emma ignored the flutter of nerves in her stomach. She'd had enough excitement for one day. "My car won't start," she said with a sigh. "I was just calling Dad to see if he could come give me a jump."

"Sounds like you've got plenty of juice. I don't think it's the battery." Ash straightened. "Pop the hood and I'll take a look."

"But…do you know anything about cars?"

He turned at that, and for the briefest moment, he seemed to hesitate. Then he grinned. "Not really, but maybe we'll get lucky and the problem will be obvious."

Emma released the hood latch and watched while he fiddled around with some wires.

"Find anything?" she called out the window.

"Not really, but give it a crank and let's see what happens."

Emma turned the ignition and got the same result. A groan followed by a whimper.

Ash slammed shut the hood and came back over to the window. "My advice is to call a tow truck. You're going to need a mechanic."

Emma took the key out of the ignition and climbed out of her car. "I'll go over to the garage and see if Jimmy has time to take a look at it this afternoon."

"Jimmy?"

"Jimmy Vaughn. He bought Metz's Garage a few years ago."

Ash nodded toward his car. "Hop in and I'll give you a ride over there."

Emma had no intention of getting into the car with Ash Corbett. He looked too good in his jeans and soft T-shirt, and her stomach hadn't stopped trembling since he showed up. "It's not that far. I can walk."

He squinted down at her. "Come on, Emma, it's hot out here. Let me give you a ride."

She gazed at the gulf for a moment as she tucked her hair behind her ears. She wasn't sure why she was so reluctant to get in the car with Ash. He was just offering to give her a lift.

Maybe that was the problem. Maybe he'd really meant it last night when he said he wanted to be her friend. But Emma wasn't sure she was ready for that. Right now the tug of attraction was a little too strong, and she wanted to stay angry with him for letting her believe he was dead. It was safer that way.

He opened the door for her and she got in. The leather seats were buttery soft and cool from the air-conditioning. "I like your car," Emma said when Ash had climbed in behind the wheel.

"Thanks." He started the engine and pulled onto the street. "You'll need to refresh my memory about Metz's Garage. It's on Fourth Street, right?"

"Close. Elm Street. Take a right at the next light."

"That's right, Elm Street," he muttered. "I don't know what I was thinking."

"There used to be another garage on Fourth Street, but it's been closed for years."

"Yeah, that's probably the one I had in mind."

Emma glanced at him, letting her gaze linger in spite of herself. In profile, he looked more like the Ash she remembered. The strong jaw and perfect nose were exactly the same and those blue eyes were still so striking against his tanned skin.

She used to tease him that he could be a movie star if he wanted, but he'd just laugh and tell her that he'd never make it in Hollywood because he wasn't any good at pretending.

When he glanced in her direction, Emma quickly looked away.

"I'm not surprised that you don't remember Metz's Garage," she said. "You always took your Porsche to a place in Corpus to have it serviced."

"Ah, yes, the Porsche," he murmured.

"You loved that car," Emma said. "What happened to it?"

"I sold it a few weeks after I left here."

"Sold it? I'm surprised your grandmother gave you the title."

"She didn't." He gave her an enigmatic look. "But you can pretty much buy and sell anything if the price is right."

Emma was troubled by that look. It seemed the more time she spent with Ash, the more she realized just how far they'd drifted apart. He was starting to look the same to her on the outside, but inside, he was a completely different man.

"Why did you sell it?" she asked.

He paused. "I needed the cash, and a car like that kind of stuck out in some of the places I found myself. I didn't want to attract attention so I decided to get rid of it. I figured Grandmother could use it to track me down."

Emma started to say something, then thought better of it.

"What?" he prompted.

"Nothing."

"You were about to say something. I want to know what it was."

"Just forget it," she said. "It doesn't matter now."

He shot her another glance. "You don't think she would have used the car to track me down?"

Emma sighed. "I don't know. Like I said, what difference does it make now?"

Ash turned back to the road. "She didn't try to find me, did she?"

Emma stared at him in shock. "You *knew?*"

"No, not until now." His features hardened as he stared at the road. "I wondered why it was so easy to disappear, but now that I think about it, it makes sense. She wouldn't want to do anything to make herself look weak."

"That's exactly what she said. It was your decision to leave. It had to be your decision to return. I'm sorry," Emma said. "For whatever it's worth, I think she realizes she made a mistake."

He gave a bitter laugh. "I doubt that. Grandmother has never been one to own up to a mistake. I just wish I'd known twelve years ago that she hadn't sent the dogs after me. It would have saved me a lot of trouble."

"And your Porsche," Emma said.

"And the Porsche."

He flashed her a smile, and for one brief moment, the years melted away.

A FEW MINUTES LATER, EMMA had dropped off her key with Jimmy Vaughn and explained the problem with her car as best she could. He agreed to tow her car to the garage and call her with an estimate when he figured out what the damages would be.

Emma climbed back into Ash's Mustang and they headed for home. The road followed the coast, and she kept her gaze trained on the passing scenery. For a moment back there, she'd felt something that she really did not want to feel. And she'd seen something in Ash's eyes that told her he'd felt it, too.

Maybe nothing else remained of their teenage romance, but the attraction was still there. For one split second when their eyes had met over smiles, the tension had sizzled between them.

After a while, Ash said, "So what have you been doing all these years?"

She turned with a frown. "What do you mean?"

"David Tobias said you'd only been working for Grandmother for a few months. What were you doing before that?"

"I worked for an insurance company in Dallas."

"And before that?"

"Before that I was in college."

He kept his gaze trained on the road. "What made you decide to quit your job and come back here?"

"For one thing, I wanted to be close to my dad in case he needed me." She paused. "And there were other personal reasons I wanted to come back."

He said carefully, "Like that guy you were with earlier? Is he one of those reasons?"

Emma turned. "What guy? You mean Rick?"

"Rick. Is that his name?" He spared her a brief glance.

"Rick Bledsoe. We went to high school together. He's a deputy with the county sheriff's department now."

"I gathered that much from the car you were in. And I assumed since you didn't appear to be under arrest that the encounter was a friendly one."

Something in his tone took Emma completely by surprise. "What are you getting at?"

He gave her a longer perusal. "I'm not getting at anything. I'm just making conversation."

"Then why does it feel like I'm being grilled?"

"Must be your imagination. Like I said,

I'm just making conversation. If you have a problem with my questions, you don't have to answer them."

Emma folded her arms. "I don't have a problem answering your questions. I have a problem with you asking them. You sound as if…" She broke off and glanced out the window.

"I sound like what?"

"Never mind. Let's just drop the subject, okay? I don't mean to be rude, but I've had a long day and I really don't feel like talking."

"Sure. Whatever."

She could tell from his tone that he was annoyed, but Emma didn't care. All those questions about her personal life…if she didn't know better she'd almost think he sounded jealous. But that would mean that he had to still care and he'd made a point of letting her know last night that he didn't. So what was she supposed to think?

Emma wanted to turn and look at him, but she kept her gaze focused on the passing scenery. They both fell silent and no one spoke until the car hit a bump and Ash swore.

"Sorry," he muttered.

Emma did turn to look at him then. "No problem. I've never heard you use that word before. You were always pretty careful about your language."

"Yeah, well, that changed once I was in the service. I broadened my vocabulary along with my horizons."

"Your grandmother told me that you spent some time in the army," Emma said. "I find that hard to imagine."

He glanced at her. "Why?"

"I just never pictured you as the military type."

His mouth tightened at the corners. "Why is that? Because of my background? You think pampered rich boys like me don't feel a responsibility to their country?"

"No, I just meant…I didn't mean to offend you," she said softly.

"I'm not offended." He lifted his hand from the wheel to rub the back of his neck. "It's just good to know what you really thought of me."

"Ash—"

"Let's just drop it, okay? I don't feel much like talking, either."

An awkward silence settled over the car once again, and Emma stared miserably out the window for the rest of the way home.

When Ash parked the car underneath the

portiere, she turned and said quickly, "Thanks for the ride."

She opened her door and climbed out, hoping that she could get inside before he caught up with her. But he blocked her way before she could open the garden gate.

"Look, I'm sorry that things got a little tense on the ride home. I shouldn't have pried into your personal life."

"And I shouldn't have questioned your patriotism. Let's just call it even."

She tried to walk past him, but he took her arm. "Emma…"

The way he said her name…the way he stared down at her…

Emma closed her eyes for a moment. "What do you want from me, Ash? Last night you all but told me I have no place in your life, and today you act as if…"

His gaze darkened. "As if what?"

She drew a shaky breath. "As if you care who I see or what I do."

"I do care. I told you last night that I want us to be friends again."

"I don't think that's a good idea. I think it would be best if you stayed away from me," she said bluntly.

"That might be hard, considering we live under the same roof."

"It's a big house. I think we can manage if we try."

She turned away again, but he still wouldn't let her go. His gaze lit on her throat, and she saw him go very still.

"What happened to you?" he asked in a strangely harsh voice.

Emma tried to keep her scar covered most of the time, but after she'd taken off her jacket earlier, the tank top she wore left her throat completely exposed.

He reached up and very gently traced his finger along the scar. "What happened?" he asked again.

"It was nothing. An…accident."

"That was no accident." When his gaze lifted, Emma shivered at the look in his eyes. "I've seen knife scars before. Who did that to you, Emma?"

She put her hand over the scar. "It doesn't matter."

"Oh, it matters. Who was it? Someone you knew?"

She shook her head. "No. I'd never seen him before. He broke into my apartment one night and attacked me. But I'm alive and that's all that matters."

"And where is he?"

He asked the question in a very quiet voice, but Emma couldn't help shivering. There was an edge in his tone that she'd never heard before and it frightened her.

"He's in prison. He'll be there for a very long time. It's over and done with and there's no point talking about it anymore. And I really wish you'd stop looking at me that way."

"What way?"

She lifted her chin in defiance. "Like you have a right to know about my personal life. You don't."

"Maybe not. But I didn't have a right to do a lot of things I've done in my life. That never stopped me."

And before she realized what he meant to do, he bent and kissed her.

Emma was so stunned she couldn't react. She didn't kiss him back, not at first, but neither did she move away.

She stood stone still as his lips moved back and forth on hers, and then when his tongue slipped inside her mouth, she opened in response.

His arms came around her and he pulled

her hard against his body. The kiss wasn't gentle, but neither was it cruel or punishing. If Emma had to put a name to the emotion, she would have said it felt a little desperate. At least on her end. Maybe she was trying a little too hard to recapture something that just wasn't there anymore.

His fingers slid into her hair and his thumbs caressed the sides of her face. His touch was so familiar then that the desperation slipped away, replaced by a bittersweet desire that tore at Emma's resolve, that ripped through the years of pain and disillusionment and reminded her instantly of how much she had once loved Ash Corbett.

He'd always known how to kiss her, where to touch her, when to whisper exactly what she needed to hear.

He'd once known her better than she knew herself, and he used that intimate knowledge now to strip away the last of her defenses.

When they broke apart, Emma's knees were weak and trembling and all she could do was stare up at him for a moment before she backed out of his arms.

"Why did you do that?"

"I didn't mean to." He looked as shaken as she was. He ran a hand through his hair and looked away. "I'm sorry. It won't happen again."

"Why?"

He couldn't meet her eyes. He kept his gaze focused on some distant object as he said, "You know why."

"Because I'm not good enough for you." She was stunned by the bitterness in her tone. "Is that it?"

Something flickered in his eyes and he glanced away. "No. Because I'm not good enough for you."

Chapter Ten

Emma hurried through the parlor, anxious to get to her room before Ash caught up with her. She heard him come in the French doors behind her and call out her name.

"Emma, wait!"

She had no intention of waiting, but as she strode into the front hall, she stopped short.

Maris and Helen had come out of the study and were standing at the bottom of the stairs. Helen saw Emma first, and then her gaze hardened when Ash came into the hall behind her.

Emma could only imagine what conclusions the woman was drawing from their appearance. There Emma stood, all windblown from the boat ride and her cheeks flushed from the sun. And from the kiss.

And Ash...she didn't dare look over her shoulder at him.

Instead Emma said as calmly as she could, "I'll be in my room if you need me, Mrs. Corbett."

She hurried up the stairs without looking back and didn't stop until she'd reached her room. Then she leaned weakly against the door and closed her eyes.

Ash could deny it all he wanted, but his lips had told her something very different. Something she'd been longing to hear for twelve long years.

He still loved her.

HELEN CORBETT WATCHED EMMA run up the stairs and then she turned without a word and walked back into the study.

Maris gave Ash a bemused look. "So you and Emma…?"

He shrugged. "We're just friends."

"It looked a little more than friendship to me," Maris said. "I've been around the block a few times. I recognize sexual tension when I see it, especially when it practically oozes out of your pores the way it was with you and Emma just now. I don't have to tell you that Mother will not pleased."

"It's none of her business," Ash said with a frown.

"That's not the way she's going to see it. Ash, if you're not careful, you could make Emma's life very difficult around here. She's a good person. I don't want to see her get hurt. By you or by Mother."

"I'm not going to hurt Emma." Although after what he'd just done, his words rang hollow. "There's nothing going on between us. We were just reminiscing about the old days."

"Is that what they're calling it now?" Maris shook her head. "I don't know why I'm bothering to talk to you about this. You'll do as you please. You always did. And besides, you're a grown man. You don't need me to lecture you on your love life." She turned down the hallway toward the study.

Ash's glance traveled up the stairs. It was all he could do not to follow Emma up to her room. But she'd been right earlier. The best thing he could do was stay away from her. He'd already let his attraction get out of hand, and now she was up there right now with the wrong idea about them. About their future.

He'd screwed up royally, but he had to believe that he could somehow fix the damage. At the moment, though, he didn't have a clue how to do that. Not without hurting her again.

"Come into the study," Maris called over her shoulder. "Mother has something she wants to talk to you about." She glanced back with a smile. "Something besides Emma I mean."

But when they entered the study, Helen Corbett acted as if she'd never witnessed the scene between him and Emma. She sat behind her desk and motioned for him to take the seat across from her.

"I asked Maris to come out here today so that we could get started on the tests," she said. "The sooner we get all this business behind us, the sooner we can start making plans for the future."

"What are you talking about?" he asked suspiciously. "What test and what plans?"

"The DNA tests," Helen explained. "They're just a formality as far as I'm concerned, but I don't want anyone questioning my judgment down the road."

He tried not to sound worried. "I don't have a problem with a DNA test, but I thought David Tobias was making the arrangements." If Tobias wasn't involved, the whole plan could come crashing down around him. He'd have more problems to deal with than Emma's hurt feelings.

"David has already made the necessary ar-

rangements. I'm just collecting the samples."
Maris went over to Helen's desk and opened
the medical bag propped on the corner. "I've
already drawn Mother's blood for comparison. Now I need some from you."

"Sure. Why not?" Ash held out his arm.

Maris snapped on a pair of surgical
gloves and removed a syringe from the bag.
"I don't remember you being the squeam-
ish type. You haven't developed a phobia for
needles, have you?"

"If I don't pass out you can take that as a no."

Maris swabbed his arm and then prepared
the vein. Glancing up with an enigmatic
smile, she said, "Don't worry. I'm very good
at what I do. You won't feel a thing."

EMMA HAD DINNER WITH HER FATHER that night.
All through the meal, she kept thinking about
Ash even though she'd promised herself
earlier that she wouldn't dwell on what had
happened between them. She didn't want her
father thinking that something was wrong. The
last thing he needed was to worry about her.

But as they stood at the sink doing the
dishes, he brought up the subject of Ash.
"Why didn't you mention last night that he
was coming home?"

"I wanted to tell you, but Helen asked me not to say anything until she'd had a chance to see him for herself. I guess there was some question as to whether he really is Ash."

"He does look different," her father said, putting away the freshly dried plates. "But I'd know him anywhere."

Emma looked at him in surprise. "You saw him?"

"He stopped by for a minute or two this afternoon."

Her mouth dropped. "Ash was here? Why?"

Her father shrugged. "He said he wanted to say hello. But between you and me…" He picked up a dripping pan from the sink. "I think he was looking for you."

"Me? Why?"

"I don't know, Emma. You tell me."

Emma concentrated furiously on scrubbing a pot. "I don't know what you're talking about, Dad. If Ash stopped by here…I'm sure it had nothing to do with me. He knew that I was running errands for Mrs. Corbett."

"Maybe he thought you'd be finished sooner. I kind of expected you home earlier, too. What'd you do today?"

Emma didn't know whether to be relieved or suspicious at her father's abrupt change of subject. "I had lunch with Laney Carroway and then we rode out to Shell Island with Rick Bledsoe."

"Shell Island?" Her father had been in the process of putting away the pan, but he paused and glanced back at her. "Why would you go out there?"

"Rick said that they go out there every so often to try and keep the vandals away." Emma finished the last of the pans and pulled the stopper out of the drain to let the water out. "Dad, do you remember that time you took me out there when I was in the seventh grade? I was doing a report on local history for school."

"Sure I remember. What about it?"

"I never told you this, but I had the strangest feeling while we were out there. Almost like a premonition. Later, when those bodies were found, I always wondered if I should have said something."

"There've always been rumors swirling around about that island. I doubt anyone would have taken you seriously. Besides, you always did have a big imagination. That's all it was, Emmy. You've never had a premonition about anything else, have you?"

"No. But whatever it was, it's made me

have a strange connection to that island all these years. That's why I went out there today. I wanted to see if I still felt that connection."

"Did you?"

Emma paused. "No, not like I did before. But I am still curious about it. Did you ever know any of the people who used to live there?"

He frowned, thinking back. "Seems to me a couple of the men worked for the Corbetts at one time."

"What were they like?"

"Hard workers, the best I remember."

Emma used the dishcloth to wipe off the counters. "Did you know anything about their religion?"

"They were pretty devout," he said. "No cussing, no drinking. I never asked for any particulars. Wasn't any of my business."

"Laney and I saw a pentagram painted on the floor of one of the houses today, and it made me remember all those rumors about sacrifices and rituals. You don't think there was anything to those stories, do you?"

"If you mean do I think those people were devil worshippers, no I don't. That's just talk. I saw a special about it the other night on TV. Some of those people they interviewed believed in blood sacrifices and had some kind of strange attachment to cats. Crazy stuff." He shook his head. "Those guys that I knew weren't into anything like that. They were good people."

"I'm sure you're right," Emma said. "It was probably just some kids fooling around out there. I saw a lot of other graffiti, too. It's just…after what happened out there, it made me wonder."

Her father's expression hardened. "I don't think you should go out there anymore if that place bothers you like that." He went over to his easy chair and sat down. He looked a little pale tonight. Emma was worried about him but she didn't want to fuss.

"I satisfied my curiosity this afternoon. I don't plan on going back out there again," she assured him as she dried her hands on a dish-towel. "You didn't forget to take your medicine today, did you?" she tried to ask casually.

"I have a bad ticker, Emma, I'm not senile."

"I know that. But I also know how you are when you get busy."

"I took my medicine," he said grumpily. "I'm fine. Just a little tired tonight, that's all."

"Maybe you need to ease up a little on the workload," Emma said. "Cut back on your hours."

"You mean I should think about retiring."

Emma shrugged. "Might be kind of nice not to have to get up and go to work every morning. You'd have time to do all the things you've always wanted to do."

He leaned his head back against the chair and closed his eyes. "Those things I always wanted to do cost money, you know."

"You've got some savings and a retirement plan. You'd be okay."

"I need a couple more years," he said. "Then things won't be so tight."

Emma knew better than to argue with him. "Just take care of yourself, okay."

"Stop worrying about me," he muttered, already half-asleep.

"Good night, Dad."

"'Night. Be careful walking home."

"I will." Emma dropped a kiss on top of his head. "Don't sleep in that chair all night. You'll have a stiff neck in the morning."

He grunted in response and Emma watched him for a moment, then showed herself out.

Instead of walking up the drive, she used the shortcut. A storm was blowing in from the gulf, and the air was heavy with moisture.

Just as she emerged from the trees, the leaves began to whisper overhead and then the rain came. She was close to the summerhouse and she decided to head for the nearest shelter.

Running through the shower, she stepped quickly into the gazebo only to realize that someone else had already had the same idea.

"Come in," Ash said softly. He sat in the dark smoking. The tip of his cigarette glowed as he lifted it to his mouth.

Emma's heart tumbled in her chest. "I got caught in the rain coming back from Dad's. I hope I'm not disturbing you."

"You're not. I'm just sitting here watching the rain."

"I didn't know you smoked." She ran a hand through her damp hair.

"I do a lot of things I didn't use to do."

His voice sounded odd, not at all like Ash's. Even the accent was different. Emma said tentatively, "I'm glad I ran into you tonight. I wanted to talk to you about something."

"Well, here I am. Talk away."

His indifferent tone threw her off. "I think we should discuss what happened today."

"Really? Because I don't see the need to go there. I kissed you, you kissed me back, end of story."

"But it wasn't just a casual kiss, Ash. You—"

"I what?" He flipped his cigarette out into the rain and stood. "What is it you think you read into that kiss?"

Emma bit her lip as tears sprang to her eyes. "Why are you doing this?"

"I'm not doing anything."

"Yes, you are. Last night you made it clear that you didn't come back home because of me. Today you grilled me about my personal life as if you were jealous of who I see. And then you kissed me…the way you used to kiss me. And now this…attitude of yours." She peered at him through the dark. "You keep sending me all these mixed signals and if I didn't know better…"

"Go on. If you didn't know better…"

"I'd think you weren't Ash," she said softly.

He moved toward her in the dark. It was all Emma could do not to back away from him. She suddenly felt very afraid.

"Maybe you just need a little more convincing." He reached up and traced a finger down her throat.

Emma jerked away from him. "Don't do that."

"Why not? You enjoyed it this afternoon." He moved in even closer.

Emma took a step back from him and felt the

wall of the gazebo behind her. He put a hand on the wood above her head and leaned in.

She moistened her lips. "What are you doing?"

He smiled down at her. "You may not be sixteen anymore but you're still an attractive woman." His eyes gleamed in the dark as he cupped the back of her neck and pulled her to him. "Come on," he coaxed. "Let me convince you that I'm Ash."

Before she could answer, he bent quickly and kissed her. His mouth pressed hard against hers as his arms tightened around her. Like earlier, the kiss wasn't gentle. But there was no desperation in it, either. Certainly no passion. It was cold and calculating, a kiss that was meant to taunt.

When Emma tried to push him away, he held her even tighter and panic welled in her chest. Images burned through her mind…of being held down…of her clothes being ripped off her body…the searing pain as the knife blade bit into her skin…

With a gasp, she pushed him away as hard as she could. He released her then and stepped back from her. But she could tell that he was still smiling and her blood went cold with fear.

"Who are you?" she asked on a shaky whisper.

"You know who I am."

Her chin lifted. "You're not Ash. He would never do what you just did."

"Are you sure about that?"

She inched toward the door, but he saw what she meant to do and he moved between her and the opening.

"Let me go," she warned. "Or I'll start screaming loud enough to wake up the whole county."

"Don't do that, Emma." His voice had gone very quiet.

Emma put a trembling hand to her mouth as she stared at him in the dark. "You're *not* Ash, are you?"

He shook his head very slowly. "No, I'm not your precious Ash. And I'm going to need you to keep your pretty little mouth shut because I have no intention of going back to prison. No matter what I have to do."

HE COULD SEE HER TREMBLING in the dark. She was terrified and he hated like hell having to do that to her. But if she kept picking at the pieces, she'd eventually put everything together on her own, and it was better that he take control of the situation and try to repair the damage as best he could.

"Who are you?" she asked raggedly. She was still afraid of him, but she hadn't run away yet. He wasn't sure if that was a good sign or not.

"Just stay calm and I'll tell you what you want to know. But keep your voice down, okay?"

He'd positioned her so that she was facing the door and he saw her cast an anxious glance over his shoulder. "Why should I believe anything you say?"

"Because if you go off half-cocked, you're only going to cause trouble for both of us. You don't want that. Come on, sit down," he said. "I won't hurt you. I won't even touch you."

She made no move to do as he said. "Who are you?" she asked again.

"My name is Tom Black."

"Where's Ash?"

He lifted one shoulder. "I don't know. Dead probably."

She gasped, on the verge of tears. "What did you do to him?"

"I didn't do anything to him. That's the God's honest truth."

"Then how do you know he's dead?" she

demanded, her fear momentarily forgotten in her anger.

"I don't know that he is dead. I've never seen him. But twelve years is a long time, Emma. Maybe you should think about giving up the ghost."

She turned away. "If you're not Ash, how did you know about the gazebo? Why do you keep coming down here?"

"I followed you here last night. I've been studying a lot of old home videos and it was pretty clear to anyone with two eyes that you had a thing for Ash Corbett. You were crazy about him. And then when we met on the road last night, I could tell you were still carrying a torch. I figured if anyone could see through me, it would be you. Especially if you got too close. So I decided to convince you that it was over between us."

"But you said things that only Ash could know."

"No, I didn't. Think back, Emma. All I did was respond to what you said."

Her eyes gllistened in the dark. "Why are you doing this?"

"I have my reasons."

"You're after Helen's money," she accused.

"No, I'm after Ash's money. His mother

left him a trust fund. It's just been sitting there all these years not doing anyone any good. I don't see the point in letting all that money go to waste, particularly when I don't have any."

"You'll never get away with this. If I tell Helen what you just told me—"

"You won't do that, though." Her breath quickened, and he said, "Relax, I'm not going to hurt you. I don't have to."

"What do you mean?"

"What do you think would happen if you march up to the house right now and tell Helen Corbett what you just learned? I'll come in right behind you and say that you made the whole thing up to cause trouble for me because I didn't return your advances. Who do you think she'll believe?"

Emma said furiously, "I'll find a way to make her believe me. You can't know everything about Ash."

"I know enough. You don't think I would have walked into this thing unprepared, do you? Face it. All the bases are covered, Emma, and you're still an outsider. You try to make trouble for me and the family will close ranks. That's what people like the Corbetts do. They protect each other. The only thing you'll accomplish by revealing the truth is to get yourself fired. And maybe your old man, too. Is that really what you want?"

"I can't let you get away with this," she said on an angry whisper.

"Why not? Who am I hurting? Helen Corbett? She's not exactly your biggest fan, in case you haven't noticed. Wouldn't it feel good to stick it to her for a change? And besides, that money doesn't belong to her. She wouldn't even miss it." He paused. "Look how happy the old broad's been to have her grandson home. If you take that away from her, she might have another stroke. You want that on your conscience?"

"You can't put this on me. You're not her grandson. This isn't right."

"But if she never finds out the truth, where's the harm?"

"She will find out. It's only a matter of time before you slip up. What about when the DNA results come back? She'll know then."

"They'll come back a match so no worries there."

Emma watched him in the dark. He could tell that she was trying to figure him out. A part of her needed to believe that he was Ash. That was the only reason she was still there.

"How can the samples match if you're not

Ash?" When he merely shrugged, Emma said through gritted teeth, "Answer me, damn it. It's the least you can do."

"A sample of the real Ash's DNA will be substituted for mine."

"How did you get his DNA?"

"Emma, just leave it alone, okay?"

Her mind was working furiously, trying to put it all together. "There's only one way you could have a sample of his DNA. If you didn't see him…if you didn't hurt him…then someone else must be helping you. Someone with access to the family, to this house." She paused. "I'm right, aren't I? You're not working alone. You never could have pulled this off by yourself. Someone has been feeding you information. Coaching you on how to act, how to speak, even how to hold your head. They told you about me, didn't they? Who is it? Who's behind this?"

"I don't know who it is. I was contacted through an intermediary."

"An intermediary? What do you mean?"

"Just what I said. A third party has made all the arrangements. He's the one I've been dealing with."

"A third party," Emma murmured. She glanced up. "It has to be David Tobias,

Helen's lawyer. She said that he'd arranged for you to have a DNA test. That's how the swap will be made, isn't it?"

He was amazed and none too pleased by her perception. "It doesn't matter. We're going to pull this off with or without your help. But if you insist on involving yourself, you'll only end up getting hurt. So for your own good, just forget we ever had this conversation."

"I can't do that. What you're doing is illegal. I'd be an accessory after the fact."

"Emma, I'm telling you, for your own good, forget we ever had this conversation."

She caught her breath. "Are you threatening me?"

"I told you I wouldn't hurt you. I meant it. I'm not a violent man."

"But you don't know what the others would do. Is that it?"

He wanted another cigarette, but instead he took a mint from his pocket and popped it in his mouth.

Emma stood quietly for a moment while she tried to digest everything that he'd told her. He had no idea what was going to happen next. If she ran off to tell Helen, how far was he willing to go to stop her?

But to his surprise, she sat down abruptly

and turned to stare out at the rain. "Did they kill Ash?" she asked after a moment. "The people you're working with, I mean."

He shrugged. "I don't know. I don't think so. I think Ash just disappeared to get away from his family. He may be still alive somewhere, but…I don't think he's coming back, Emma."

She continued to watch the rain. "Who are you?"

"I told you my name."

"I mean…who are you?"

He sat down beside her. "I'm nobody. Just a guy who's never caught a decent break in his whole life."

Her head jerked around. "You think that justifies what you're doing?"

"No. I'm not making excuses. I'm just trying to answer your question. You wanted to know who I am. I was born in Louisiana. My mother died when I was twelve and I was in and out of foster homes until I turned eighteen. I spent some time in the military and when I got out, I went back home to Louisiana. I started up a construction business in New Orleans, but the storm wiped me out. I lost everything. I evacuated to Houston with a lot of other folks, and I eventually ended up in Corpus Christi. I guess someone saw me one day and thought I looked like Ash. The next thing I know, I'm being offered a quarter of a million dollars just to convince an old woman that I'm her long-lost grandson."

She turned back to the rain. "You said earlier that you were in prison."

"I spent eighteen months in a state pen for a burglary I didn't commit."

"You expect me to believe that you were innocent with what you're trying to pull?"

"I'm telling you the truth. Whether you believe me or not is your business. But there's one thing you *have* to believe. Whoever set this up has a lot of money and a lot of influence. Public records have been changed, official documents forged, you name it. They've made damn sure my identity would never be questioned, and if they find out that you know the truth…"

She looked at him then and even in the dark he could see the glint of fear in her eyes.

"You have to keep your mouth shut, Emma. Do you understand?"

"If I go to the police—"

"The police can be bought. Everybody can be bought for a price," he said bitterly. "I found that out the hard way."

"No one held a gun to your head and

forced you to do this," Emma said. "Or did they? You said earlier that you would do anything to avoid going back to prison. Did they somehow threaten you?"

He hesitated. Even after everything he'd told her, she was still clinging to some hope that he was the man she wanted him to be. He had to look away from her probing gaze. "They offered me the money," he said flatly. "That was enough."

"That explains why you're doing it," she said. "But what are they getting out of it? How does Ash's return benefit anyone? I would think just the opposite. He was always Helen's favorite. Why would anyone else want him to come back?"

"I'm not just here to convince her that I'm her grandson," he said. "I'm also here to convince her that I have no interest in Corbett Enterprises."

"I see." She seemed to ponder that piece of information for a moment. "Pamela Corbett told me that Helen has never changed her will in all the years that Ash has been gone. He's still in line to inherit controlling interest in the company upon her death."

"Or at any time she decides he's ready to

take the reins," he said. "I'm here to make sure that she knows he'll never be ready."

"Then the person who has the most to gain from all this is Wesley," Emma said. "But I never thought he would be the type to perpetrate a scam like this, especially on his own mother. He's always been kind and generous to my father and me."

"Loyalty has its rewards," Ash muttered. "I agree that Wesley has the most to gain, but I don't exactly trust the other brother, either. How well do you know Brad Corbett?"

"Not nearly as well as I know Wesley."

"Where do you think he stands with Helen in terms of her will?"

"I have no idea," Emma said. "But since he's now second in command at the company, I assume he would only inherit controlling interest if something happened to Wesley—" She broke off.

"What is it?"

"I just thought of something. When I was leaving Wesley's office today, I saw Brad and Pamela getting off the elevator together. They looked as if they'd been caught in a compromising position."

"So? Even if they're having an affair it doesn't make them guilty of anything else."

He rubbed the back of his neck. "Look, Emma, we could sit here all night speculating about who sent me. But the only thing that concerns me at the moment is what you plan to do about it."

"I don't know yet."

"Then you're not going to the police? Or to Helen?"

"I said I don't know," she said angrily. "I can't just let you get away with this. What kind of person would I be?"

"A survivor," he said grimly. "Isn't that what we all are?"

She lifted her chin. "Yes, but there's a limit to what some people can live with." She stood. "I need some time to think. If everything you've told me is true, then it's not just my father's job I have to worry about. He could be in danger because of what I know. And if I don't talk—"

"No one will get hurt. It's an easy choice, Emma."

"Maybe for you. But I have a conscience. And I despise you for putting me in this position," she said coldly.

Chapter Eleven

Emma spent a sleepless night, and by morning, her options were no less muddy. Even if she went to Helen and told her what she knew, there was no guarantee that she would believe her. Helen was stubborn and now that she'd convinced herself that the man living under her roof was her grandson, she would not be easily dissuaded. And according to Ash, the DNA evidence would support his claim.

Ash.

She still couldn't think of him as anyone else.

How easy her life had been twenty-four hours ago when all she had to worry about was a man who no longer loved her. Now she and her father could be in danger, and Emma didn't know what to do about it.

She considered calling Rick Bledsoe, but she couldn't stop thinking about what Ash had told her. Anyone could be bought for the right price. Could she trust Rick?

By the time she headed downstairs, she was no closer to solving her dilemma. She couldn't do anything to jeopardize her father's life. But how could she stand by and do nothing?

She had to tell Helen. She couldn't *not* tell Helen. The woman had a right to know what was happening under her own roof. The longer Emma let it go on, the more damage would be done to everyone concerned.

But when she walked into the study, her resolve fled the moment her gaze met Ash's. He'd been standing at the window looking out at the lawn, but he turned when she walked into the room. Their gazes connected, and her heart fluttered unexpectedly. After everything he'd told her, she still found him attractive. How could she not? He looked so much like Ash.

"Good morning, Emma."

The masculine voice took her by surprise because Ash hadn't spoken a word. She tore her gaze from his and glanced toward Helen's desk. Wesley was perched on the edge, sipping a cup of coffee.

"You're late," Helen said imperiously from behind her desk.

"Actually, she's early." Wesley set aside his cup and smiled. "Unless you normally have the poor woman coming in at the crack of dawn."

"I didn't think you would need me before eight," Emma said. "I apologize."

"Don't apologize for keeping decent hours," Wesley said. "Mother will think she can have you at her beck and call twenty-four hours a day."

"Don't speak as though I'm not even in the same room," Helen snapped. "Now that you're finally here, Emma, there's something I want to discuss with you."

"Actually, there's something I want to talk to you about, too." Out of the corner of her eye, she saw Ash move away from the window. She didn't know where he'd gone to until she felt his presence behind her.

"Before you and Mother get embroiled in business details, I wanted to tell you that I saw your dad this morning, Emma." Wesley's blue eyes regarded her over the rim of his cup. "He wasn't looking well. Are you sure he's taking care of himself?"

Emma's heart twisted in agitation. Was the mention of her father a coincidence or something very deliberate? Was Wesley the mastermind of the scam? He had the most to gain if Helen changed her will, but Emma found it hard to believe that a man who'd stepped in and paid for her father's medical expenses could be the same cold man who'd deceive his own mother.

But what was it Ash had told her last night? Loyalty has its rewards. Maybe that was why Wesley had paid the medical bills and gotten Emma this job. He was counting on their loyalty as his reward.

"I think you should see to it that he takes it a little easier," Wesley said. "We don't want him suffering a relapse. He's too valuable to this family. And to you, of course."

Emma nodded, but her mouth had gone dry with fear.

"What was it you wanted to tell me?" Helen said with a frown.

Behind her, Ash touched her shoulder. She almost jumped out of her skin. "I…nothing. It can wait."

"Then sit down and let's get to work. My birthday is coming up. I was just telling Ash and Wesley that I'd like to celebrate the way we used to. We haven't had a real party in this house in years. It's high time we did. But the kind of event I have in mind will take a great deal of planning and we're already behind schedule. I'll need you to work overtime, Emma. Are you going to have a problem with that? You'll be compensated accordingly, of course."

Emma nodded. "I don't mind overtime."

"Good. Then if you two will excuse us, we have a lot to do."

Wesley bent and kissed his mother's cheek. "A party is a great idea. Just don't you overdo it, okay?" On his way out of the room, he paused beside Emma and said in a low voice, "I'm glad you're here to keep an eye on her for me. And as for your father..." He touched her arm. "Don't worry. I'm sure he'll be fine."

She turned to find Ash watching her. He nodded almost imperceptibly before he left the room behind Wesley.

"YOU DID THE RIGHT THING," he said a few minutes later when he caught Emma alone.

She pulled away from him and said coldly, "Don't you dare speak to me that way."

He frowned in confusion. "What are you talking about?"

"Don't act like we're in this together. You've put me in an impossible position. You know I'll do anything to protect my father.

And I may decide yet that the best way to do that is to go to the police."

"You'd be making a mistake," he said. "The police can't help you, Emma. I told you last night, they've got all the bases covered. The only way you and your father will be safe is for you to say nothing. Just let it happen and no one gets hurt. And no one will blame you for doing what you have to do."

That might be, Emma thought. But she didn't like being manipulated and bullied. She didn't like having her father threatened. Maybe it was high time she showed a little backbone and started fighting back.

A FEW DAYS AFTER THE ENCOUNTER with Ash, Emma found herself alone in the house. Helen had been driven into Corpus Christi for a doctor's appointment and Ash had gone off somewhere after lunch.

From a window in the study, Emma had watched his car disappear down the drive and then she'd hurried up to the third floor where his room was located. The staff quarters were downstairs so Ash had the top floor to himself. Emma had never been in that part of the house before, but she knew where to find his room. She used to watch his window from her own bedroom in the caretaker's cottage. Sometimes she would catch a glimpse of his silhouette moving back and forth in front of the window, and later, once they'd become close again, he would flash a light as a signal that he was thinking about her.

She tried to put those memories out of her head. She needed to forget about Ash. The real Ash, at least. After twelve years, he was never coming back. What she had to concentrate on now was getting her and her father out of this mess in one piece.

She found Ash's room and tried the door. It was unlocked and, glancing down the hall in both directions, she slipped inside. Pausing just inside, she looked around, wondering where she should start. There had to be some evidence of who he really was in this room. Some shred of proof that she could take to Helen and to the police that would make them believe her in spite of the DNA results.

The room was just as Emma had always imagined. Clean, neat and sparse. But the simple lines of the furnishings were deceptive. Everything in the room was expensive. Helen had hired a designer from Dallas to redo Ash's suite when he first moved in and every couple of years thereafter.

The only thing that ever changed in her room at the cottage were the posters on the walls that had reflected her taste in music and movies during various stages of her youth.

Moving as quickly as she could, she searched through the bureau drawers and the nightstands, and finally his closet. After nearly half an hour, she hadn't found one thing that tied the occupant of the room to Tom Black. Or to Ash Corbett for that matter. She should have known he wouldn't be so careless as to leave evidence of his true identity lying around in his room, but it had been worth a try.

Emma left his room frustrated but still determined to find the evidence she needed. Sooner or later he was bound to slip up. And when she had proof, she would be able to fight back.

For now all she could do was watch and wait.

OVER THE NEXT FEW DAYS, Emma made it a point to check in on her father every day. Helen had her working impossible hours, but Emma still found the time to at least drop in for a few minutes before bedtime each night.

He wasn't looking well these days and Emma was very worried about him. He'd been putting in a lot of overtime as well, getting the grounds ready for Helen's big party. He hired additional labor as he needed it, but Emma knew that he still did a lot of the work himself.

One night after dinner, she checked his calendar and reminded him that he had a doctor's appointment the following day.

"I'd forgotten all about it," he admitted. "I've got some plants being delivered from the nursery. I'll have to cancel the appointment."

"Don't do that, Dad. Your health is more important than any plants. Maybe you can reschedule the delivery."

"No, I can't. The exotics have been special ordered just for the party. They'll have to be tended to immediately."

"I can't imagine that a few hours would make a difference, but even if it does, you can instruct one of the workers what to do when they come. Don't miss your appointment, Dad. I want you to have a checkup. I'm worried about the kind of hours you've been keeping."

"I'm fine, Emmy, stop fussing over me." He dropped the magazine he'd been reading and gave her a long appraisal. "You're the one I'm worried about. Look at you. You're skin and bones. And you don't look like you've been sleeping all that well, either."

"I'm fine. We're all under the gun these days." She came over and sat down across from him. "When I used to climb up that tree by the terrace and watch Helen's parties from a distance, I never had any idea how much work goes into an event like this. It's exhausting."

Her father was still scrutinizing her. "Are you sure that's all it is?"

"What do you mean?"

"It seems to me you've got something on your mind these days, Emmy. What is it? Maybe I can help."

Tears burned her eyes and Emma quickly looked away. Time and again she'd been tempted to tell him about the imposter. He was the one person that would believe her without question.

But Emma also knew that he would insist she tell Helen and the police about the scam. If she didn't, he would. He would probably scoff at the threat of danger, but she knew firsthand that sometimes those threats were carried out.

Open your mouth and I'll slit your throat.

She'd done as she was told that night. She'd kept her mouth shut and hadn't fought back, but this time would be different. First she had to make sure the odds were in her favor. She couldn't take a chance on anything happening to her father because he was all she had left.

EMMA TOOK THE SHORTCUT BACK to the house that night, and as she came out of the trees, she glanced at the summerhouse. She could see the faint silhouette of someone standing in one of the arched openings and the orange glow of his cigarette as he lifted it to his mouth.

Emma stood there for a moment, watching from the darkness, and then she turned her back on the gazebo and headed for the house. He caught up with her as she was walking through the garden. Emma heard the squeak of the gate behind her and a shiver slid up her spine.

She turned and watched him move toward her. "What do you want?"

He said nothing as he advanced toward her. The night was very still. The only sound in the garden was the trickle of the fountain and the pounding of Emma's heart. She told herself that she wasn't afraid of him, but she was. Not because she thought that he would hurt her. But because he reminded her so much of Ash.

Even after everything he'd told her, Emma

couldn't stop the flutter of her heart every time she saw him. She wondered what that said about her character, that she could still be physically attracted to a man who lacked a decent moral fiber.

She lifted her chin and glared at him through the darkness. "I told you to stay away from me."

"I just wanted to ask you a question."

She could see him clearly in the landscape lights. His features were at once strange and disturbingly familiar. "Did you find what you were looking for?"

Emma frowned. "What are you talking about?"

"You searched my room the other day. Did you find anything?"

Emma started to deny it, but then she shrugged. "No. Not yet. But I will. And the moment you slip up, it's all over."

His eyes narrowed at her threat. "Emma, be careful. If they suspect that you know who I am, you could be in a lot of danger."

"So you said. But I don't know why I should trust anything that comes out of your mouth. For all I know, your threats are just another way to keep me quiet. I can't believe I bought into it."

"You bought into it because you know it's true." He glanced off into the darkness. "I'm sorry you're caught in the middle of this. if I could undo this thing right now, I would. But it's too late for that."

"No, it's not. If you went to the police, they'd have to believe you. It would all be over, but then…you'd have to face up to the consequences of your actions, wouldn't you?"

"I'm not worried about that. Not anymore."

"Then what's stopping you?" Emma demanded.

"There's no evidence of a conspiracy. I've never talked to anyone but David Tobias. And he's not a fool. There's no way he'll let me implicate him. It'll be my word against his."

"But all the things he told you about the Corbetts and about Ash…the videotapes and the photographs that he gave you—"

"Long gone," he said grimly. "We're not dealing with an amateur, Emma. He knows how to cover his tracks. The best thing either of us can do is let this thing play out. I'm making progress with Helen. She knows how I feel about Corbett Enterprises. I wouldn't be surprised if she makes the changes to her will before her birthday."

"And then what?" Emma asked coldly. "You'll take Ash's money and disappear?"

He shrugged. "Eventually. And then you can forget you ever knew me."

"I won't forget what I've done," she said bitterly. "You've made me a part of this filthy scheme and I won't be able to move on as easily as you seem to think. Every time I look at Helen—"

"You'll see a cruel, vindictive old woman who drove off her only grandson. Don't waste your pity on Helen Corbett."

"You're just trying to justify what you're doing," Emma said. "And I don't care what you say, I think you'll do just about anything to keep from going back to prison."

"The way you look at me is worse than any prison," he said harshly. "Don't you get that?"

Emma stared at him in shock. "What?"

He closed his eyes briefly. "I hate what I've done to you. I hate what I'm asking you to do."

"Why?" she asked almost fearfully.

"Because I think I'm falling in love with you," he said and, turning, he walked out of the garden without another word.

Emma stood there for the longest time staring after him. She didn't want to feel anything but revulsion for what he'd just told her, but a part of her...

God help her, a part of her had responded in a way that frightened her.

"I ASSUME YOU HAVE A suitable dress for the party," Helen said a few days later.

Emma looked up from her desk in surprise. "I hadn't thought that I would attend."

"Of course, you'll attend. There'll be a million last-minute details that you'll need to oversee."

Hardly the invitation Emma had always dreamed of, but she felt a thrill of anticipation anyway. Her first Corbett party. She would be working, of course, but at least she would *there*, in the midst of it all, and not observing the glamorous festivities from the branches of an oak tree.

"I'm sure I can find something," Emma murmured. "I'll drive into the city the first chance I get."

"Bring me the receipt," Helen said. "It's a business expense so make sure you get something appropriate."

In other words, don't show up in something cheap and tacky and embarrass her, Emma thought.

THE PARTY WAS ONLY A few days away, and the house was abuzz with the elaborate preparations. Emma had been working harder than ever, which was a blessing in some ways. She didn't have much time to consider anything other than the myriad tasks that were relegated to her.

But after her conversation with Helen, she'd managed to sneak in a day of shopping. She made the arrangements ahead of time with Laney Carroway, and the two of them drove all the way to Houston for a full day of shopping.

For hours they combed the posh boutiques in the Galleria, and even though the price tags were a bit overwhelming, Emma fell in love with almost everything she tried on. She'd never seen so many beautiful dresses. But she was especially drawn to a white Grecian chiffon that flowed beautifully when she moved.

It was exactly the kind of gown she'd always imagined herself wearing to make a grand entrance down the magnificent curving staircase in the Corbett mansion. In her fantasy, Ash would be at the bottom of the stairs gazing up at her. He would take her hand and lead her into a glittering ballroom where they would dance the night away in each other's arms.

In reality, of course, she would be working her butt off that night, but Emma didn't care. She might never again have the opportunity to wear such a gown.

When she got home late that night, she went straight up to her room to put away her purchases. Removing the gown from the protective bag, she walked over to the full-length mirror and held the dress up to her. Slipping the hanger over her head, she turned first one way and then the other, making the gown swirl like froth at her feet.

"Beautiful."

She whirled to find Ash standing in her doorway. She clutched the dress to her body, even though she was fully clothed underneath. It was just the idea of him in her room...watching her so intimately...

Emma pulled the hanger over her head and tossed the dress onto the bed. "What do you want?"

"You were gone a long time," he said. "I was starting to get worried about you."

"I had a lot of shopping to do." Then she added coolly, "Not that it's any of your business."

He smiled as he walked into the room.

Emma said angrily, "I didn't invite you in."

"You didn't tell me to leave, either, I noticed."

She folded her arms and glared at him. "Please leave."

"I will in a minute. Let me see what you bought."

Before Emma could stop him he plucked the dress from the bed and held it up. "Nice," he said admiringly. "I can't wait to see this on you. You'll be the most beautiful woman at the party."

Emma snatched the dress away from him. "Don't touch my clothes. And don't talk to me that way."

He looked amused. "What way?"

"Don't stand there and act like there's something between us. There's not and there never will be."

"Are you sure about that, Emma?"

She lifted her chin. "Do you think I actually believed what you told me the other night?" She gave a bitter laugh. "I know what you're doing. It's just another attempt to buy my silence."

"Is that really what you think?"

She couldn't help noticing that his eyes

were very blue tonight. Very blue and very intense. She tried to turn away from his gaze, but he took her chin and brought her back around to face him.

"I told you the truth the other night. It's the first honest thing I've said in years. I'm falling in love with you."

She jerked away from him. "Stop it."

"Why does that scare you so much?"

"I'm not scared."

"Yes, you are." His gaze burned into hers. "I can see it in your eyes. You're afraid of me. But not because you think I'll hurt you. You're afraid that if you let yourself, you'll feel something for me, too."

"That's never going to happen," she said angrily. "You're not the kind of man I could ever fall in love with."

His features hardened almost imperceptibly. "Because I'm not Ash?"

Emma sighed. "What do you want from me? I've done what you asked me to do. I've kept my mouth shut. Why can't you just leave me alone?"

"Because you're you," he murmured. His fingers slid back into her hair and for the longest moment, they stood in silence.

Emma told herself that she needed to

distance herself from his touch. She had to remember who he was. And who he wasn't. She couldn't let herself get caught up in the moment, in the desire burning in his blue eyes.

But when he bent to kiss her, she didn't try to stop him. Her eyes fluttered closed and she started to tremble. *I can't fall in love with him,* she thought desperately. *I can't let him get to me.*

His kiss was tentative and gentle, but the passion simmered around the edges, ready to explode the moment she responded.

She tried not to, but the way he kissed her…it wasn't the way Ash had kissed her. It wasn't the way anyone had ever kissed her before.

Ash had been a boy, her first love. Gorgeous, charming, charismatic. But part of Emma's attraction had always been the fantasy. He was a Corbett. The very epitome of what she'd always wanted but could never have.

This man was all too real. He was unscrupulous and cunning, a con artist and a liar. He'd been to prison and to probably a thousand other places that Emma wouldn't even be able to imagine. He'd involved her in a scheme that could possibly endanger her life and that of her father's. And yet Emma made no attempt to push him away.

Instead, she leaned into the kiss and parted her lips.

He groaned into her mouth, the other hand coming up to weave into her hair. He held her face still as his lips moved over hers, and Emma couldn't stop shaking.

When he finally broke the kiss, he pulled her into his arms and buried his face in her hair. "I'm sorry," he said on a ragged whisper. "I shouldn't have done that. But I've wanted to for so long…ever since I saw you on the road that first night."

Emma didn't know whether to believe him or not. She couldn't even believe her own emotions. Maybe the only reason she wanted him was because he looked like Ash. After all these years, she still couldn't say goodbye to him.

She pulled away and looked up at him. "What are we going to do?"

"Nothing," he said and released her. "We have to be careful. We can't let this happen again. Not until it's over."

"And when it's over," she said softly. "What happens then?"

He didn't say anything, but Emma knew

the answer. When it was over, he'd be going away. Back to prison…or to someplace where the Corbetts wouldn't be able to find him.

Either way, Emma would not be going with him.

Chapter Twelve

Helen's birthday dawned bright and clear, with only a mild breeze blowing in from the gulf. The day couldn't have been more perfect, Emma decided as she supervised the setup in the kitchen.

Earlier that morning, the family had all gathered in the dining room for a private birthday breakfast. Afterward, Wesley and Pamela had left in separate cars, with Brad and Lynette following closely on their heels. Ash disappeared, too, but Maris lingered to make sure that Helen went straight upstairs to rest for the entire today.

When she came back down, she found Emma in the front parlor working with the florists. Most of the furniture had been moved out of the huge room, and a temporary dais had been installed for the orchestra. The corners were filled with potted palms and tree ferns creating a tropical oasis that spilled out onto the terrace.

And flowers were everywhere. Orchids and roses and lilies of the valley. The fragrance hung thick and heady in the air-conditioned room, a scent that took Emma back to her childhood and the hours she'd spent perched in a treetop dreaming.

Outside, more flowers banked the terrace and pool, and the trees and shrubbery had been strung with an intricate arrangement of white lights.

Maris looked around and smiled. "You've done an impressive job, Emma. The house looks wonderful."

"Thanks, but I can't take the credit. Your mother did most of the planning. I only executed her wishes."

"Oh, you did far more than that. I know how much work goes into one of these things. Mother never would have been able to pull it off without you." She touched Emma's arm. "I can't tell you how much I appreciate everything you've done for her. We all do."

Emma was discomforted by the woman's effusive praise. "I'm only doing what I'm paid to do," she said.

"I don't really believe that, but even if it's true, it still means a lot to have someone in this house that we trust." Her hand was still on Emma's arm and her grip tightened ever so slightly. "I won't say anything more because I don't want to embarrass you, but I just wanted you to know that your efforts haven't gone unnoticed or unappreciated."

She smiled but something in her eyes sent a shiver up Emma's spine. *Your efforts haven't gone unnoticed or unappreciated.*

Was she the one? Emma wondered suddenly. Could Maris be the one who had arranged for an imposter to come into her Mother's home?

Wesley was the obvious suspect because, on the surface, he seemed to have the most to gain, but she hadn't discounted Brad, either, especially now that she suspected he was having an affair with Pamela. Emma wouldn't put anything past Wesley's wife, including masterminding a conspiracy that would replace her husband with her lover at the helm of Corbett Enterprises.

But until that very moment, Emma had never considered that Maris might have her own reasons for wanting her mother to change her will.

INSTEAD OF THE GRAND ENTRANCE she had always dreamed of, Emma came down the back stairs that night. She was dressed in her swirling white gown and the silver high heels that matched the beaded trim around the empire waistline.

Even without the entrance, Emma's blood quickened in excitement. She made a quick run through the kitchen and serving areas, and then slipped into the parlor, where the first guests had already gathered.

The air-conditioning had been turned down low so that the terrace doors could be thrown open to the night breeze and the party spilled outside. The orchestra was already playing, but no one was dancing yet. Helen was still receiving her guests, along with Wesley and Brad, both handsome and distinguished in their tuxedos.

Emma scanned the room, wondering where Ash was. And then she spotted him in one of the corners with a slim blonde in a slinky black dress. Something sparked in his eyes as his gazed lingered on Emma, and the blonde turned to see who had captured his attention.

Her dismissive gaze moved past Emma and then she turned back to Ash. He smiled and nodded at whatever she was saying, but his eyes remained on Emma.

She moved out of his line of sight. He had said they needed to be careful, so why was he looking at her that way?

And why was she letting a conman manipulate her? He didn't love her. He was only using her, and the sooner Emma got him out of her life, the better.

But as the dancing began, she couldn't stop the prickles of jealousy that stole over her when he took the blonde in his arms. She was clinging to him, laughing and flirting and thinking that he was Ash Corbett, heir to a vast fortune. Would she be as interested if she knew the truth?

Why not? You are, a little voice taunted her.

But Emma didn't want to be reminded of her weakness. She moved toward the door, thinking that she would make another check of the kitchen, but someone touched her shoulder and she turned to find Ash staring down at her.

"Dance with me."

Emma frowned. "I don't think that would be a good idea. You said yourself we have to be careful."

"I am being careful." He smiled and glanced around, as if they were merely exchanging pleasantries. "Would the real Ash ask you to dance?"

Emma hesitated. "Probably," she admitted.

"My job is to be Ash," he said. "He would ask you to dance. It's expected. But if you keep avoiding me, someone might get suspicious."

"Or someone might think that I've finally learned my place," Emma said.

He took her hand and with a gentle tug, pulled her into his arms. "This is your place. At least it could be."

"And where would I end up?" Emma asked. "On the run from the law?"

His arms tightened around her. "You don't need to be afraid. I won't let anything happen to you."

"Something has already happened to me." She glanced around the room, wondering if Helen was watching them. "You've made me care about someone who doesn't even exist. You're not Ash. I don't even know if you're Tom Black. But when this is over, I'll still be the same person I've always been. I'll still have to live with myself."

She pulled out of his arms and left the dance floor. She saw Helen then. The woman was flanked by well-wishers, but her gaze was on Emma.

Emma nodded and smiled and hurried out of the room. As she crossed the front hall, she glanced back, but Ash had already disappeared into the crowd.

Lynette Corbett came out of the room then and smiled when she saw Emma. "Hello, Emma. You look very pretty tonight."

"Thanks, so do you."

And she did. The icy blue gown complimented her blue eyes and blond hair. Diamonds glittered around her wrist as she lifted a hand to smooth back her hair.

"I was looking for Brad," she said. "He seems to have disappeared. You didn't see him come out here, did you?"

"No, I'm sorry." Emma hadn't seen Pamela Corbett, either, and the woman would be hard to miss in her scarlet beaded dress. She wondered if Brad and Pamela were together somewhere.

Lynette bit her lip. "Do you think we could go someplace more private and talk?"

The request took Emma by surprise. "I was just about to check on the champagne—"

"This won't take but a moment. There's something I feel compelled to say to you, Emma. It's for your own good."

Emma had barely spoken two words to

Lynette Corbett her entire life, and she didn't quite know what to say to her now. She started to make another excuse to slip away, but then she shrugged and said, "We can go into the study."

Lynette moved past her and led the way down the hall. When Emma followed her into the study, Lynette glanced both ways before sliding the doors closed. She turned to Emma, her expression troubled.

"This is probably none of my business, but I saw you and Ash dancing just now. I couldn't help noticing the way he looked at you…the way you looked at him…"

Emma's heart skipped a beat. "It was just a dance. There's nothing going on between us."

"I think you mistake me," she said softly. "I don't disapprove. I don't care that you're in love with Ash. I would wish you two every happiness except…that's not possible in this family."

"Mrs. Corbett, I'm not in love with Ash."

"Yes, you are," she said sadly. "I can see it on your face even now. You're in love with him and you have no idea how much that makes me pity you."

Emma was stunned into silence for a moment.

"This family has terrible secrets, Emma."

A knot of fear formed in Emma's throat. "What are you talking about?"

"If you marry Ash, you'll become a Corbett. Those secrets will become part of you. If you try to get away from them, you could end up like Ash's mother."

Emma gasped. "What are you saying?"

"Get out now," Lynette said desperately. "Get out and don't look back."

"Mrs. Corbett—"

Lynette glided to the doors, but before she slid them apart, she glanced back at Emma. "We never had this conversation. For both our sakes, keep your mouth shut and just walk away while you still can."

EMMA REMAINED IN THE STUDY for several long moments, trying to compose herself. Lynette's warning had shocked her deeply and Emma knew that her emotions would show on her face.

But she also knew that she couldn't stay away for too long. She would be missed and people might start asking questions. So she left the study and made her rounds once again, performing her duties as best she could, but inside, she trembled with fear.

What on earth had Lynette meant by terrible secrets? She hadn't been talking about Ash because she seemed convinced that he *was* Ash. So convinced that she'd warned Emma away from him.

What secrets did she mean then?

After a while, Emma managed to slip outside for a few minutes to catch her breath. Her mind tumbled with questions and she didn't know what to do. She was involved in something that went much deeper than the scam. The Corbetts were a powerful family, and if she somehow crossed them…

She shuddered as she walked across the terrace and out into the deeper shadows beyond. Standing at the base of the oak tree, she glanced back at the house. How many times had she watched from this very spot and dreamed of belonging to that glittering throng inside?

The Corbetts had seemed like golden people to her back then. Like royalty that could only be admired from afar.

Now she realized that the fairy lights and the flowers and the flowing champagne created nothing more than an illusion. A beautiful shroud that covered a terrible darkness beneath.

"I wondered where you'd gone off to."

Emma turned at the sound of his voice. At that moment, she was almost glad that he wasn't Ash. Because the look in Lynette's eyes when she warned Emma away from the Corbetts had been more frightening than anything Tom Black had told her yet.

She shivered in the warm night air. "I need to get away from here."

"Sure," he said. "We'll slip away for a few minutes and go for a drive."

"No. I mean…forever. I can't stay here. I can't be a part of this."

His voice lowered in concern. "What happened?"

"I can still walk away," she said desperately. "I won't say anything about what you're doing because…I don't care anymore. I just want out of here."

He looked around, assuring himself that they couldn't be overheard. "It's not that simple. If you leave without any warning or reason, it'll look suspicious."

"I don't care. I'll disappear," she said. "Like Ash did."

"What about your father?"

"He's not a part of this. If I'm gone, he'll be safe."

"If they suspect you know too much, what

makes you think they won't use your father to get you back? They're ruthless people, Emma. They'll do anything to get what they want. Besides, you're not the type to run away. You never have been."

"You're wrong." She wrapped her arms around her middle as she moved away from him. "Why do you think I left Dallas? I was running away from what happened to me there. I'm not strong and I'm not brave. I just want to be happy," she said. "I want to fall in love with someone normal and have a family. I don't need all this. I never did. I only thought I did because…"

"You were in love with Ash."

"I was in love with a dream. I can see that now. It wasn't real. None of this is real." She drew a shaky breath. "When I was little, I used to climb up this tree and watch parties like this and I wondered what it would be like to be one of those beautiful people inside. But I never really thought I could be a part of it until one night I fell out of this tree right at Ash's feet. And he said—"

"What took you so long."

HE SAW THE SHOCK REGISTER on her face a split second before the anger took hold. "How did you know that? Who told you?"

"Emma—" He tried to take her arm, but she jerked away from him.

"There's only one person who could have told you that. Where is he? Where's Ash?"

"Right here, Emma."

"What? No! You're not Ash. You said..." She trailed off and closed her eyes. "Why? *Why?*"

"I have my reasons. I can explain everything, but not here. It's too dangerous."

Her eyes filled with tears. She put a trembling hand to his face. "Ash?"

"Yes. It's me."

"I can't believe it. I thought you were dead. All those years..."

"I know."

"You let me think you were dead. Why?"

"I had to. Emma...there's so much you don't know. So much that *I* don't even know. But if what I suspect is true, we could both be in a lot of danger."

"From whom?"

"From someone in my family. I meant what I said earlier. They're ruthless people who will do anything to get what they want. They're not above murder, Emma. Not by a long shot."

"Murder?"

"Shush." His gaze shot to the terrace. "Keep your voice down."

"If they're that dangerous, why did you come back?" Emma asked.

"I came back because you did."

Her eyes went wide with yet another shock. "You came back…because of me?"

His voice hardened. "Someone had to be here to protect you. I knew your father was sick and you had no idea what this family is capable of. I had to do something."

"But…I don't understand. Why not just come back? Why pretend to be an imposter—" Emma broke off as laughter sounded nearby.

Ash pulled her into the shadows and whispered against her ear, "We can't talk here. I'll come to your room later."

And then he slipped away, leaving Emma alone and trembling in the dark.

EMMA HAD CHANGED OUT OF HER gown into jeans and a casual shirt and was standing by the window staring out into the dark when the soft knock sounded on her door. She crossed the room and drew it open a crack. When she saw Ash in the hallway, she stepped back so that he could enter.

He came inside and closed the door, and for the longest moment, neither of them spoke.

Emma had been wondering what she would say to him. How she could ever believe him. Could she really trust that he was Ash?

He smiled slightly as if he knew exactly what she was thinking. "You got your braces off the summer before Grandmother sent me away to boarding school," he said. "Your favorite band that year was the Smashing Pumpkins. I got you one of their CDs for your birthday."

Tears filled Emma's eyes, but she still said nothing.

"When you turned sixteen, I bought you a tiny gold heart pendant with both of our names engraved on the back. Kind of lame, I'll admit, but I never claimed to be original."

Emma touched her throat where the heart had once lain against her skin. "I loved that necklace. I wore it for a long time after you left. I finally took it off when I realized you were never coming back, but I didn't get rid of it. I still have it, along with everything else you ever gave me."

He reached up and stroked his knuckles down her face. "You shouldn't have kept it. You should have thrown it away. You should have been married with kids of your own by now. If anyone deserves to be happy, it's you."

"How could I be happy thinking you were dead?"

He closed his eyes. "You don't know how many times I wanted to call and let you know that I was all right."

"Why didn't you?"

"I couldn't. It was too dangerous."

"Dangerous? Ash, what's going on? I don't understand any of this."

"It's a long story," he said and moved past her to the window. "And I don't even know where to begin."

"I do." She walked up behind him. "Twelve years ago. Start with the night you left here."

She saw his shoulders rise slightly as he drew a breath. "Grandmother and I had it out that night. She gave me an ultimatum. She said if I didn't break things off with you, she'd fire your dad and make sure that neither of you ever set foot on Corbett property again. And I believed her. I knew she was capable of that and much worse."

He turned from the window, his expression bleak. But there was an edge of anger in his tone. "You have to understand how she operates, Emma. It's not about love with her, it's about control. She has a knack for finding a person's weakness, and once she has power over you, you never get away. She won't let you. My father tried. He stayed gone for a while, but then she found a way to lure him back, and in the end, he liked being a Corbett more than he loved my mother and me. Grandmother couldn't control my mother and that's why she hated her. She made her life miserable, Emma, and I didn't want that for you."

"So you left."

"I left and I was young enough and naive enough to think that I could go off on my own and start a new life, just like that. I wasn't going to be like my father. I was never coming back here. And once I was settled with a good job, I was going to send for you."

"Why didn't you?" Emma said softly. "I would have gone to you, you know. Wherever you were. It wouldn't have mattered."

"I was counting on that. But then something happened to make me realize that it didn't matter how far away we got, my family was always going to find me. I would never have any peace as long as my last name was Corbett."

"So you changed it?"

He shrugged. "Not quite as simple as that. I got rid of the Porsche because I didn't want Grandmother using it to track me down. I traded it for an old beat-up Ford and kept the previous owner's title and registration. I thought that would be enough, but someone found me. My car was forced off a bridge one night and I was left for dead."

Emma gasped. "Helen would never do that. She's a stubborn old woman, Ash, but she loved you."

"It wasn't Grandmother who wanted me dead."

"Then who was it?"

"I can't prove it, but I've always thought it was Wesley. No one else had as much to gain from my death as he did."

"There's no way it could have been an accident?"

Ash shook his head. "That truck deliberately rammed my car. There was no one else on the road. He must have followed us out of town that night."

"Us?"

"Someone was in the car with me, a guy I'd met on a job site in Shreveport. He had a lead on another job in New Orleans and the two of us were driving down there together. After we went over the bridge, I managed to pull him out of the water, but he was already dead. He'd gone through the windshield and his face was all cut up. There was nothing I could do for him. He'd told me once that he didn't have any family. He'd been orphaned when he was twelve years old. There wasn't anyone that was going to miss him or come looking for him, so I took his ID and from that moment on I became Tom Black."

"That's why you never called me," Emma said. "Or wrote to me."

"I couldn't. I couldn't take a chance on Wesley finding out that I was still alive. I didn't want to put you in any danger. If he knew that I hadn't died in that crash, he could have used you to get to me, and I wasn't going to let that happen. When I heard that you'd moved away from here, I was tempted to get in touch with you in Dallas. I even drove up there one day. But by then it had been years since I left. I didn't think you'd still want to hear from me. And I was still worried that Wesley might somehow find out. So I parked across the street from your apartment and waited for you to come out. I watched you get in your car and drive off, and then I left."

Emma closed her eyes. He'd been so close that day. If only she'd known.

"And then a little while ago, I heard that you'd moved back here. That you were actually living in this house. I couldn't *not* come back then. You had no idea what this family is capable of. I had to make sure you were safe."

"I still don't understand why you couldn't just come back as Ash?"

"Because Wesley was still around. I didn't intend for him to see me. All I wanted to do was get word to your dad so that he could persuade you to leave. But then I was spotted on a job site, and a few days later, David Tobias approached me."

"And he believed that you were Tom Black?"

"He had me checked out first."

"But there must have been photos of the real Tom Black."

He shrugged. "A mug shot that didn't even look like the real Tom Black. Tom was a drifter. He didn't leave much of a paper trail other than his prison record. Besides, they didn't dig too deeply because they were already convinced that I was dead."

"And as long as you remained dead, you weren't in any danger."

"Nor were you."

"So they approached you about posing as Ash to get Helen to change her will."

"That's why I think it's Wesley. He had every reason to believe that I was dead and out of the way, but Grandmother didn't. And she refused to change her will. He could either wait for her to die and hope that the others didn't challenge him, or he could arrange to have the company turned over to him with Grandmother's blessing."

"But you don't know for sure that it *was* him," Emma said.

"I don't know that he was the one who tried to kill me, either. But someone did."

Emma sat down on the edge of the bed, suddenly exhausted by the night's events and by everything she'd just learned from Ash. "Why did you tell me that you were Tom Black? Why didn't you want me to believe that you were Ash?"

"Because I didn't want you getting the wrong idea about us. I needed a way to make you keep your distance."

"Is that the only reason?"

He turned from the window. "That's the

main reason," he said. "But a part of me wanted to know if you could love someone like me. You always put me on a pedestal, Emma. You had this fantasy of who you wanted me to be, and I guess I just wanted to know if you'd still be attracted to me if I didn't have this house or the Porsche or the Corbett name."

Emma got up and walked over to the window where he still stood. She wrapped her hand around the back of his neck and pulled him down for a kiss. Slowly she moved her mouth back and forth against his until she felt his response and then she drew away.

"Does that answer your question?"

Chapter Thirteen

"Damn, my hands are shaking," Ash muttered as he struggled with the buttons on her blouse.

"Here, let me." Emma unfastened her blouse and slipped it slowly down her arms. Then she undid her bra and as it fell away, she heard the sharp intake of Ash's breath.

"You're beautiful, Emma."

She was starting to tremble, too. "I'm not sixteen anymore."

"Neither am I. I'm not the same man that left here twelve years ago. In a lot of ways, Ash Corbett really is dead. I've done some things in the past that I'm not really proud of. Are you sure you want to get mixed up with a guy like me?"

She kissed him again, a long, deep, intimate kiss that made her heart pound in anticipation. She tugged at the tail of Ash's shirt, and he broke the kiss long enough to yank it over his head and toss it aside.

He sat down on the edge of the bed and pulled her between his legs. "I've thought about this since the moment I first saw you on the road."

"I've thought about it for years," Emma confessed. "But now that you're really here, I'm...nervous."

"Why? It's just me."

"That's the problem. It's you."

"Don't do that," he said softly. "Don't put me back on that pedestal. I don't belong there."

"Old habits die hard. No matter what you call yourself, you'll always be Ash to me. I'm not talking about the money," she said quickly. "I'm not talking about this house or the fancy car you used to drive. I'm talking about the way you make me feel."

"You don't think you make me feel the same way?"

"I don't want to disappoint you."

He gave a low laugh. "That's not going to happen."

"How do you know? It's been a long time since we were together and I haven't exactly gained a lot of experience in that time. I haven't been with a lot of men."

"I haven't been with a lot of women."

She smiled. "Now why don't I believe that?"

"It's true. And it doesn't matter anyway because none of them were you."

"Ash." She sighed his name as he drew her to her. They kissed for a long time, and then his mouth skimmed down her throat, touched her scar briefly, then found her breast.

Emma's knees trembled as she buried her fingers in his arm. She couldn't believe this was happening. She couldn't believe that Ash—the real Ash—was finally home and they'd found each other again. Their bodies could still create the same old magic.

He unbuttoned her jeans and slid them, along with her underwear, down her legs and Emma stepped out of them. Then she pushed him back on the bed and moved over him, trailing kisses along his chest and down his flat stomach.

He was different, Emma noticed. He'd always had a great body, but now he had the muscle definition of a man who'd worked hard for a living. A man who knew how to use his hands.

She unfastened his jeans and he helped her slide them off. And then there was nothing between them but twelve years of loneliness, and even that faded as their bodies touched for the first time.

He sat up and pulled her onto his lap. Wrapping her legs around his hips, he lifted her onto him and Emma's breath quickened. Her heart pounded hard against her chest as she moved slowly at first, and then more desperately as time and memories slipped away. Nothing mattered but that moment....

"Ash…"

"I know," he whispered on a ragged breath. "Just let it happen."

She wrapped her arms around him and held on tight as her climax exploded over her. He was right there with her, and he fell back against the bed, still shuddering as he pulled her with him.

SOMETIME LATER THEY'D CLIMBED between the sheets and Emma lay in the crook of his arm, her head resting on his chest. "You can't leave again," she whispered furiously. "You can't just disappear the way you did last time, Ash. I can't lose you again."

His arm tightened around her. "When I leave here again, you'll be going with me."

"But how? You're still in danger. I don't want Wesley using me to track you down."

"I think it'll all be over soon. Grand-mother said at breakfast yesterday that she's ready to make some changes to her will. Once Wesley becomes her heir, he'll have what he wants. He won't have a reason to come after us."

"But he tried to kill you. He won't just forget about that."

"I can't prove it was him. Besides, he tried to kill Ash. As long as he thinks I'm Tom Black there's no reason for him to come after me."

Emma splayed her hand on his heart. The rhythm was steady and reassuring. "When do you think it'll happen?"

"She said she was setting up a meeting with David Tobias in a day or two, and then she'll call the family together and make a formal announcement."

"And then it'll be over," Emma said. "Everyone gets what they want."

"I already have what I want," Ash murmured.

Emma lifted her head to kiss him. It was a long, soulful kiss that opened her heart and bared her emotions. A kiss that was, in some ways, more intimate than lovemaking.

"I love you," he whispered against her mouth.

"I love you, too."

EMMA WOKE UP SOME TIME later to find him dressed.

"Where are you going?" she asked drowsily.

"I have to get back to my room before everyone is up and about and someone sees me leaving your room." He bent and kissed her. "Go back to sleep."

She rolled onto her back and stared up at him. "All this sneaking around…it's kind of like old times, isn't it?"

"It won't be for much longer," he promised. "Now get some rest. You don't want people to wonder what you were up to all night."

He crossed the room and, drawing the door open, glanced into the hallway. Then he quickly stepped outside and pulled the door closed behind him.

EMMA GOT UP AT HER REGULAR TIME, showered, dressed, and was headed down the stairs to the study when a scream tore through the house.

She paused at the top of the stairs, her blood going cold. And then she started running toward the sound. It had come from the direction of Helen's suite and as she hurried down the hallway, she saw that the door was open.

Helen lay unconscious on the floor and

Theresa Ramon knelt beside her. The woman looked up in horror as Emma came running into the room. "I found her like this when I brought her breakfast. I don't think she's breathing."

"I'll call 911," Emma said, crossing to the phone. Just as she was dialing the emergency number, Ash came in.

"What happened?"

Emma tuned out Theresa's frantic explanation as she gave the 911 operator the requested information.

When she hung up, she went over to Ash, who was kneeling on the other side of Helen, checking for a pulse.

"Is she…?"

"I can feel a pulse, but it's faint," he said grimly. "How long before the paramedics get here?"

"Ten minutes maybe. They're on their way."

"I don't know if that's going to be soon enough." He checked her pulse again, and then Emma heard him whisper, "Hang on, Grandmother. Help is on the way."

THE PARAMEDICS ARRIVED IN eight minutes, and Maris came in right after them. She checked Helen's vitals, her expression as grim as Ash's. Once Helen was loaded into the ambulance, Maris climbed in to ride with her to the hospital. "I'll call as soon as I know something," she promised.

They watched as the ambulance disappeared down the drive and then Emma turned to Ash. "Ash, I'm so sorry. What do you think happened?"

"I don't know. Maybe the excitement of the party was too much for her."

"She's tough," Emma said. "She'll pull through this."

He shook his head. "Not this time. There's only so much that even Grandmother can take."

Emma put her hand on his arm. "Ash…she didn't change her will yet."

His gaze darkened as he stared down at her. "I know. But I can't think about that now. I have to get to the hospital."

EMMA BUSIED HERSELF ALL DAY overseeing the cleanup from the party. Ash called once to say that Helen's condition was critical. She'd suffered another massive stroke and wasn't expected to pull through. Emma had asked if there was anything she could do, but Ash had said no and quickly hung up.

Emma didn't want to have bad thoughts

about a woman who might be lying on her deathbed, but it seemed to her that Helen's collapse had pulled Ash back into the family. She'd seen how worried he was about Helen. It was only natural. No matter how cruel and vindictive, she was still his grandmother. His own flesh and blood. Emma didn't resent his concern. What niggled at her was the knowledge that if Helen died, Ash would inherit everything. Would that change how he felt about Emma?

It seemed ghoulish and cold to be thinking about the consequences of Helen's death when she was still very much alive. And she was a fighter. If anyone could pull through this, it was Helen Corbett.

Emma called the hospital late that afternoon, and then she walked down to the cottage to have dinner with her father. The two of them talked a little about Helen's condition, but mostly it was a quiet, somber meal. Emma left soon afterward. She was anxious to get back to the house in case Ash returned.

As she emerged from the trees, her gaze went automatically to the summerhouse. She saw the orange glow of a cigarette, and her heart quickened. Ash was back.

She hurried over to the gazebo and

stepped through the door. It was very dark inside. She could barely see his silhouette. He had his back to her as he stared out into the darkness.

"Ash." She walked over and put her hand on his shoulder.

His hand came up to covers hers, and she let out a breath.

"I didn't know you were back. How's Helen?"

"She died nearly an hour ago," Wesley said, his hand clamping around Emma's wrist. "And now your precious Ash is a very rich man."

Emma tried to back away from him, but he held her fast. Getting up from the bench, he slowly turned to face her. She couldn't see his face, but his eyes were gleaming in the dark. They looked almost feral.

She tried not to panic. He didn't know that she knew. Maybe she could bluff her way out of this.

"I'm sorry about your mother."

He laughed. "No one's sorry about Mother."

"That's not true—"

"Emma, Emma." He shook his head. "You still don't get it, do you?"

"Get what?" She tried to pull away from

him, but he wouldn't let her. "Please let me go. You're hurting my wrist."

"Am I?" He released her then and held up his hand. "There. You're free as a bird."

But Emma knew better than to run. Not until she had a better shot at getting away. She still wanted to believe that she could talk her way out of this.

"Where is Ash?" she tried to ask casually.

"Still at the hospital with the others. He's putting on a good show, I must say. Already taking charge. You should see him, Emma. He's acting like a real Corbett."

Emma didn't say anything. She was too busy worrying about how to get away from him.

"Another day or two and it would have been mine," he said. "All of it. Amazing how important timing can be."

"Nothing has to change," Emma said. "Ash doesn't want Corbett Enterprises. He's not interested in the money."

"Don't fool yourself, Emma. Everyone is interested in that kind of money. Because it can buy what everyone wants. Power."

"Not Ash—"

"Yes, even Ash," he said with a snarl. "He's a Corbett, Emma. Nothing is ever going to change that. He'll be a Corbett...until the day he dies."

Her heart quickened at the menace in his tone. "Except...he's not really a Corbett, is he?" she whispered.

"You know about that?" He laughed. "You don't think I'm that stupid, do you? Of course, he's Ash. I told you the other day, I knew who he was the moment I laid eyes on him, I don't care what he calls himself."

"Then why—"

"Why did I hire him to pretend to be himself? You know why. So that he would get Mother to change her will."

"But you were never going to let him walk away, were you?"

"You're starting to figure it out now, aren't you? But I think you have yet to realize your part in all this."

She tried to inch toward the door. "What are you talking about?"

"Do you think we really just bumped into each other that day in the lobby of your building? I knew where you worked, where you lived. I knew that if I got you back here, Ash would be right behind you."

"You used me to get to him," she said, her voice trembling.

"That was the main reason I wanted yo back here, yes. But, Emma…" He lifted a hand and stroked her cheek. "I've had my eye on you for years."

Her skin burned beneath his fingers and she jerked away from his touch. He grabbed her and hauled her up against the wall. His eyes gleamed in the dark; his breath was hot against her face. Emma tried to turn away. "Let me go."

"I can't do that. Because you've got something I need."

"Don't—"

"You can give me power, Emma. The kind money can't buy. The kind of power that someone like you can't understand. Mary didn't understand it, either. No one did. But it's a power like no other."

Horror dawned on Emma as she realized what he was saying. It was him….

Wesley Corbett was the killer.

He had been killing for years, and now he intended for Emma to be his next victim.

He had her pinned against the wall. She couldn't move. She couldn't scream. Tears rolled down her face.

Don't do this! she silently pleaded, but there was no compassion in him. He was too far gone for that.

Emma felt the prick of a needle in her arm and then a moment later, her knees collapsed as everything around her went black.

SHE AWAKENED TO MORE DARKNESS, but as everything began to come back to her, Emma knew exactly where she was. She was in the old stone church on Shell Island. He'd laid her on some sort of altar. And suddenly she understood the sensation she'd had years ago on the steps of this church. It had been a premonition of her own death.

She tried to move her arms and legs. She wasn't tied down, but as she struggled to get up, the after effects of the drug made her dizzy.

Staggering to her feet, she tried to make her way to the door, but the room spun wildly around her. She put out her arms, trying to steady herself, and after a moment, she felt stronger.

She stumbled to the door but it was locked. Whirling, her gaze lit frantically on the long windows. If she could find something to stand on, she could pull herself up to the window.

Her head still reeling, she managed to drag one of the old pews over to a window. As she used the tail of her shirt to remove the shards of glass, it occurred to Emma that this was a little too easy. Where was Wesley? Why hadn't he tied her up? He had to have known that when she came to, she would try to escape.

Unless he thought that the drugs would keep her out longer.

Emma heard the lock in the door turn. She worked frantically at the glass, but she knew she'd never be able to get out of the window in time. He'd see her and come after her. She needed more time.

Hurrying back over to the makeshift altar, she lay down and closed her eyes.

The door closed behind him and she heard his footsteps on the stone floor. And then she could sense him standing over her. A moment later, she felt the blade of a knife against her throat.

For a moment, she was back in her apartment in Dallas with her assailant lying on top of her, ripping at her clothes. She felt that same helpless terror as the knife pressed against her neck.

And then as he bent over her, Emma's hand came up and she slashed him across the face with the shard of glass she clutched in her hand.

Stunned, he stumbled backward, blood gushing between his fingers as he clutched his cheek.

Emma rolled off the altar and ran toward the door. She was still dizzy, but the drug was starting to wear off. She could make it to the door. She had to.

She flung it open and lunged outside. The night air hit her in the face and helped clear her senses. She hesitated for only a moment and then dashed toward the beach.

THE BOAT WAS TIED UP AT the pier, and Emma crawled on board, trying desperately to locate the key or a weapon. She found nothing but a heavy flashlight and she gripped it in her hand as she climbed back up to the pier.

She heard him, then, crashing through the underbrush. He was coming after her and coming fast. The boat would be the first place he'd look, but he wouldn't stop there. The island was tiny and there was no way off. He wouldn't stop searching until he found her. Emma's only hope was to find someplace where she could take him by surprise.

Avoiding the path, she made her way back to the house that she and Laney had explored the day they'd come to the island. The floorboards creaked ominously as she stepped through the front door, but there was a far greater danger lurking outside.

Pressing herself against the wall, she tried to control her breathing as she waited.

It didn't take long. She heard his footsteps on the porch and a moment later, the door opened. She waited until he was inside and then swung the flashlight against his head as hard as she could.

He grunted as he landed hard on the floor and grabbed Emma's foot, pulling her down with him. She turned, gasping when she saw the blood dripping from his face. She'd done that to him.

"You bitch," he spat and dragged her toward him.

Emma kicked him hard in the face and when he released her ankle, she scrambled away from him and jumped to her feet. Turning, she fled down the hallway to the back room, but when she tried to slam the door closed, he was already there, blocking her way. He flung the door against the wall and stood silhouetted in the opening.

Emma glanced around frantically. There was only one window and he was closer to it than she was.

When he saw that she was trapped, he

started laughing. The knife gleamed in his hand as he slowly started toward her.

"You've got something I need, Emma. They all had something I needed."

"Don't do this," she whispered.

"I have to. It's like money, Emma. Once you taste it, you can never get enough of it. Mary was my first. And you'll be my last. At least for a little while. Until it comes back."

He started across the room toward her. The floorboards creaked beneath his feet and then gave away altogether. Emma watched in stunned belief as he crashed through. She wanted to draw a breath of relief, but already he was pulling himself up, his eyes blazing with rage.

Emma rushed through the door and down the hallway. He was behind her. She could hear him stumbling through the house, his bloodlust making him invincible.

He caught her on the porch. Emma fought him with every ounce of her strength, but even with the blood pouring from his face, he could still overpower her. He flung her down the porch steps. As Emma hit the ground, she heard something snap and a searing pain shot up her leg.

She tried to get up but she couldn't. She

tried to crawl away, but he was already standing over her. His blood dripped onto her face as he leaned down and grabbed her hair.

"You have no idea how much I'm going to enjoy this," he said.

"Wesley!"

His head lifted in surprise.

"Get away from her!" a voice shouted from the dark.

Wesley paused for just a split second before he swung the knife downward.

The blade never touched Emma. A gunshot sounded and then another. Wesley fell backward without a sound.

Ash came running over and knelt at her side. Emma flung her arms around his neck and held on tight. For a long moment, she couldn't say anything.

"It's okay," Ash whispered. "It's all over." He smoothed his hand down her hair. "We have to get you to a hospital."

"I think my leg is broken," she finally managed. "But I hurt him, too," she said furiously. "I wasn't going to die without a fight."

"You did great." He picked her up and Emma clung to him.

"How did you know I was here?"

"When I couldn't find you at home I got

scared. I went looking for Wesley. His boat was missing, and I had a strong feeling that this was where he'd brought you."

"You had a premonition," Emma said.

"I just knew you were in danger," he said. "And I had to find you because I can't live the rest of my life without you."

"I love you, too," she whispered.

A little while later they were in a boat headed back to the mainland. Emma lay on the floor as she watched Ash steer them back to safety. Every once in a while he would glance down at her and their gazes would connect in the dark.

She still couldn't believe everything that had happened. His grandmother was dead. Wesley was dead. And now Ash was in control of the Corbett fortune.

But it wasn't until much later in the hospital that she was able to talk to him coherently about their future. Her leg was set and she was floating comfortably on a haze of pain medication.

He sat on the edge of her bed, holding her hand. He hadn't left her side since he'd taken her away from the island.

"You have a lot of responsibilities facing

you now," she said. "I want you to know that I understand if you…if things change between us."

He squeezed her hand. "I never wanted those responsibilities. I never wanted any of this."

"But you can't just walk away. Too many people are counting on you."

"I realize that. And I'll do what needs to be done. But no matter what happens, I want you with me, Emma. I can't get through this without you."

She lifted a hand to caress his face. "I still can't believe you're here, that we're together. What if I wake up and find I've just been dreaming?"

He bent and kissed her. "The next time you wake up, I'll be right beside you. I'm never leaving you again because I love you too much. I don't know how I lived all those years without you."

"I love you, too," she whispered. "Always have. Always will."

After a while, she closed her eyes and drifted off to sleep. She dreamed of Ash and the future they would have together. She dreamed of a fall wedding and the birth of a beautiful baby girl. She dreamed of Christmases and birthdays and a golden anniversary with their children and grandchildren gathered around them.

And when she finally awakened, Ash was right there beside her.

* * * * *

New York Times *bestselling author*
Linda Lael Miller is back
with a new romance featuring
the heartwarming McKettrick family
from Silhouette Special Edition.

SIERRA'S HOMECOMING
by Linda Lael Miller

On sale December 2006,
wherever books are sold.

Turn the page for a sneak preview!

Soft, smoky music poured into the room.

The next thing she knew, Sierra was in Travis's arms, close against that chest she'd admired earlier, and they were slow dancing.

Why didn't she pull away?

"Relax," he said. His breath was warm in her hair.

She giggled, more nervous than amused. What was the matter with her? She was attracted to Travis, had been from the first, and he was clearly attracted to her. They were both adults. Why not enjoy a little slow dancing in a ranch-house kitchen?

Because slow dancing led to other things. She took a step back and felt the counter flush against her lower back. Travis naturally came with her, since they were holding hands and he had one arm around her waist.

Simple physics.

Then he kissed her.

Physics again—this time, not so simple.

"Yikes," she said, when their mouths parted.

He grinned. "Nobody's ever said that after I kissed them."

She felt the heat and substance of his body pressed against hers. "It's going to happen, isn't it?" she heard herself whisper.

"Yep," Travis answered.

"But not tonight," Sierra said on a sigh.

"Probably not," Travis agreed.

"When, then?"

He chuckled, gave her a slow, nibbling kiss. "Tomorrow morning," he said. "After you drop Liam off at school."

"Isn't that…a little…soon?"

"Not soon enough," Travis answered, his voice husky. "Not nearly soon enough."

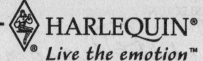

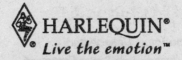

HARLEQUIN®
Presents

The world's bestselling romance series...
The series that brings you your favorite authors,
month after month:

Helen Bianchin...Emma Darcy
Lynne Graham...Penny Jordan
Miranda Lee...Sandra Marton
Anne Mather...Carole Mortimer
Susan Napier...Michelle Reid

and many more uniquely talented authors!

Wealthy, powerful, gorgeous men...
Women who have feelings just like your own...
The stories you love, set in exotic, glamorous locations...

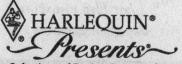

HARLEQUIN®
Presents

Seduction and Passion Guaranteed!

HPDIR104

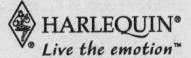

Harlequin® Historical
Historical Romantic Adventure!

*Imagine a time of chivalrous
knights and unconventional ladies,
roguish rakes and impetuous
heiresses, rugged cowboys
and spirited frontierswomen—
these rich and vivid tales will
capture your imagination!*

*Harlequin Historical . . .
they're too good to miss!*

Silhouette

SPECIAL EDITION™

Emotional, compelling stories that capture the intensity of living, loving and creating a family in today's world.

Special Edition features bestselling authors such as Susan Mallery, Sherryl Woods, Christine Rimmer, Joan Elliott Pickart— and many more!

For a romantic, complex and emotional read, choose Silhouette Special Edition.

Silhouette®